It Will Be QUICK

Karl Drinkwater

Organic Apocalypse

IT WILL BE QUICK / Karl Drinkwater

karldrinkwater.uk

ISBN 978-1-911278-17-7 (Paperback)
ISBN 978-1-911278-18-4 (E-book)

To my dog, Toby. We lay together on the grass as I read books of stories, and I told you that one day I would write my own. You died before I succeeded. Long gone but never forgotten.

CONTENTS

Fire In The Hole

THE SHOP'S NAME WAS DISHONEST. Not everything cost a pound. And a second lie hid amongst the masses of cheap batteries and bulbs and paper plates presented in tidy packets and sparkly, bright colours, as if anything plain or ugly would be ignored. How she wished that was true.

She reached the shower gel and bubble bath aisle, but a group of teen girls messed with makeup down there. Any one of them could have been her, twenty years ago, stood with her own friends, pretty and noisy and tactless, and there was no way she could walk near them, no way she could face these echoes, she knew they would stare and whisper. Or worse.

Back then she had dressed like them too, and now felt the drag of her unflattering clothes, layers for covering up rather than showing off. At least the weather was cooling and she didn't look so strange with her jacket hood up all the time.

She bypassed them by taking the next aisle. Toys. Things for smaller hands than hers. Jigsaws and puzzles and model tanks and plastic tea sets and a doll that could cry. Beyond that was the baby stuff, the nappies and dummies. She walked even quicker, averted her gaze to the hard vinyl floor, wanting to be out of here, each aisle a trap, like the shop was made out of bars.

Crowded lines of people crammed at the tills. If she squeezed past them without buying anything it would draw attention. People might think she was a shoplifter. Their stares and thoughts would burn into her.

Nearby were gardening tools, and lumpy bags of birdseed. She snatched one. That was a good idea. She could watch the birds land, and peck. They would be glad, she was sure. It was cold. Without her they might die. She grabbed an extra packet. They were worth it. Only a pound. One of the honest things.

She joined the queue. The person in front hadn't washed; their body odour lingered each time she was forced to enter the space they vacated. Instead of looking up, she sorted the change in her cold, numb hand, largest coin to smallest. Easy as long as she concentrated on not dropping them. But value didn't match size. Fifty pence was bigger than a pound. Ten pence pieces were bigger than twenties. You couldn't trust how things looked on the outside.

And now the coins were in order, but she kept prodding them as if they weren't until she could place the seed on the conveyor belt. There were no dividers and the gaps weren't big enough between her birdseeds and the next person's bottles of juice that rolled on their sides. People should control their juice. Always they let their things impinge. That was a good word, something she still remembered from school. Like the empty beer bottle someone smashed outside her flat this morning. Like body smells. Like other people. They all impinged. A soft g in a hard word.

Because she would not look up until it was time to pay, would not focus on anything but the small coins in her palm, she missed the start of the commotion. She only noticed when people left their places in the queue. An old man had fallen. Knocked over a display of lollipops. A crowd formed around him. She picked up snippets of words. He had just been coming into the shop. He had seemed fine. Could he hear? Are you okay? Is that blood on his nose? He landed badly. But there are no good landings if you faint on a hard surface. Full baskets were left on the floor as tripping hazards. She did not want to press in with the others. But no one was serving, even the till woman was trying to help. So many people.

She looked at the baskets, wondered if she should move them, be helpful, but one was not a basket. It was a buggy with three wheels. And in it was the most adorable face, the baby trying to put its own hand in its mouth, and when it saw her it smiled. It smiled at *her*. And she would have knelt and said hello to it, even if that also meant talking to the parent, but the parent was the first one to kneel by the old man who was in a bad way, definitely a bad way, it was all safe and fine and no one was looking and the baby was alone and it smiled at *her*. It had only been seconds since the fall. She would move the baby out of the way. The draught, see? Only move it. Leaving the seed on the conveyor next to the invasive orange juice, coins placed in her pocket with a noisy jingle that made her wince, just moving the buggy and expecting the mother to look at any second, or someone to tell her off – she would explain it to them, you can't be arrested for being helpful, this lovely baby smiled at her because of the draught because it needed her to do something. Two steps, was that far enough? The door was open. It was an automatic one but because of the crowd it kept juddering open again each time it tried to close, uncertain about the problem, not sure what to do, but it was sunny outside, a better place to wait where no one would trip, and although it was an entrance to the shop and not an exit no alarms sounded as she propelled the buggy out and turned right and walked down the street, pushing hard so the baby laughed and people got out of her way. This was just a good deed, they would be grateful to her, and she looked down at the baby and it still smiled. The blanket had pulled away from one leg, she covered it again, the pudgy foot, the tiny toes, six months old maybe, and she did that without stopping. She turned right again, out of sight of the shop, on the road with the travel agents and the estate agents, and there was no time to look for other agents because she thought she heard raised voices from the main street. Or it might be traffic. How could a mother leave her baby? A baby trusted, it was honest, it depended on the mother, and if you betray that trust, what then? What then? You don't deserve it. You don't deserve that love. It wasn't fair that those who deserved it didn't look after – yes, a definite shout from behind, she turned right a third time at the vinegar-stinking chip shop, small road but uphill, harder to push, small can be heavy, small can be more valuable, and it curved past parked cars and vans that hid her after she crossed to the other side.

And only now did she realise what she'd done.

They would say it was a bad thing, but they were wrong. She was just being kind. And she took another corner, because up here were fewer shops, fewer people. There was a bus stop ahead but that was too slow. She would have to wait. Stand there until people looked at her and the shouting found her and impinged on her and the baby. She passed an antique shop, had to go into the road because of the old tables on the pavement, no shelter there, nor in the sandwich shop that looked old too, and after another few roads there would be the new supermarket, always busy, and car parks of people, and ... and yes, cars. On the corner. You could rent cars there. Walking distance of the train station, easy for people. She hadn't driven since she sold her own car, couldn't afford it any more, and no need when she liked walking, but she knew what to do. She always knew what to do.

"You're my baby," she said. And still it smiled.

THE RENTAL SHOP WAS NOT really like a shop. A counter with a computer, and some chairs, and some carpet tiles, and some posters. No aisles to browse or shelter behind.

"Can I help you, love?" the older woman at the computer asked. Then she seemed surprised, that first-time-look, you get used to that, must try not to seem so nervous, why look nervous with a baby? It makes other people edgy.

She struggled to get the buggy through the door. Set it in the corner, out of sight of the window. Knelt and kissed the baby. It liked kisses. Then she covered its kicking leg again, and it made her laugh, and the woman at the desk laughed. They all laughed, it was good.

"I'd like a car please. Can I have one now?"

"Economy, compact, or intermediate?"

"Any. We want to visit my cousin."

"That's nice. You're lucky. We're often booked out in the week, but I've got a new Renault. There's no baby seat, though."

"It's okay. This lifts out, fastens ... I know how to do it."

"Really? I haven't seen one like that."

"I'm not a liar."

"No, I didn't mean that, sorry ... How long do you need it for?"

"Two days? Yes, two days. Stay with her tonight. She lives in Rhydyfelin. No, Llandysul. Yes, Llandysul."

"So you'll bring the car back here? It's possible to drop it off somewhere else."

"No, here."

Baby wanted something. She had nothing. Not even birdseed. But she could buy food in a petrol station. Just have to get away. She took her purse out.

"Please, how much will it be? I could pay with cash from the machine on the corner."

"Oh, sorry, we can't do that. It has to be a debit or credit card. Normally credit, but we're a franchise, so I can bend the rules a bit."

"Oh. Yes. My card. Here you go. It has my name on it."

"And your driver's licence."

"Oh."

"Do you have it with you? We'll need to put the details in the DVLA site along with your National Insurance number and postcode, then we get a code. Just so we can check there are no convictions."

"Convictions!" She took one step towards the door. She could leave with baby. They didn't have her name yet.

"Driving convictions. Are you all right?"

"Oh, yes. I haven't got any convictions. I'm a good driver. Very careful. I even have my licence here ... have all the papers in my bag, always ..."

She removed the driving licence and handed it to the desk woman. A siren wailed outside. Police or fire, getting nearer. They could not find her already. They would say she was wrong, take her baby away. She knelt, kissed the baby's cheeks, pinched them gently, rosy red. They would not take her baby. But the vehicle passed on the main road while she knelt out of sight. Yes, it had been a police car. It did not mean it was for her. She must behave normal. The counter woman was staring at the licence, then at her.

"It's an old photo," she explained.

"Sorry, I didn't mean ..."

"I'm thirty-three now."

"Chloe. That's a lovely name."

"Thank you. My baby needs food. I must go soon."

"Well, you're in luck. You've got one of the old licences with the paper. Can't get these now. So no need to go to the DVLA site. The deposit will be £250. Can you enter your pin here, and sign this? Read over the agreement first."

Chloe skimmed the paperwork. Too many words and clauses. A potpourri bowl on the counter smelt of sickly sweet perfume. Overpowering. She scribbled her mark at the end of the form but made it lean left instead of right. It might confuse people later. Entered the numbers in the machine. A lot of money. Almost all her money. Deposits were expensive.

"That's all done. Here's the key and paperwork. It's the blue car in the car park behind."

"This isn't a key."

"Well, the car's keyless. This is the clicker for the doors. Have you not driven recently? There's no handbrake either, just a button. If you're not okay with –"

"I'm okay with that. Yes."

Commotion erupted on the street. People moving more quickly. Staring. No, she imagined it. Must go.

"When you leave the shop go right, down the alley to the car park."

"Yes. Thank you."

"Lovely baby. He or she?"

The blanket was blue. "He. I love him very much."

"Aw. What's his name?"

"It is ..." She knelt and touched his face. He was dribbling. She used a tissue from her bag, wiped his mouth. "I must go. The family are waiting."

She didn't look back. Out the door. Every car that went past – were they looking? Someone on a phone, they might be reporting her. All seeking a woman and her baby. Too early for the news, but she was glad to get out of sight.

The alley was potholed and she had to wheel around the depressions. Cars waited just beyond, as promised. It hadn't been a lie. But so little time. Couldn't breathe until she was away from here. Far away.

You pressed a button on the clicker and the doors unlocked. The car beeped. She knew which one it was. Blue.

The buggy did not come apart. That had been a lie. She took the baby out and lay him on the front seat next to her. The buggy folded, went in the back. The seatbelt was no good for her baby, but she fastened it anyway after wrapping him warm in his fleecy blue blanket. She turned baby so part of him was under the seatbelt. It was okay. She could put a hand on him. She could look at him, watch him as she drove. He would be warm and safe. Get away. Get food and water. Breathe deep then.

The car smelt of cleaning chemicals and did not need keys. It started for her. The magic clicker must have made it work. She put the clicker in her bag, left it on the floor in front of baby. It would not be lost.

The button for the handbrake was not so good, though. The car was strange. Jerky start until she got used to it. She had to use the mirrors, but the angle was good and she only saw road, so it was okay. People stopped and looked at her as the car swerved. She cursed. Wished the car would go smoother. Then it did. When she drove people could not see the baby next to her. She smiled down at it, but it was sleepy. That meant it was happy with its mother. She knew he would be. And she was just a woman driving out of town, not going near the main street, not slowing, not looking. Just a woman getting further away. A woman with her baby, and it loved her.

SHE KNEW WHERE TO GO. Whenever possible she kept one hand on her baby. Only to reassure it, that it was solid, still there, real warm flesh and blood. Her flesh and blood. It was happy and asleep.

At the garage she parked at the side. Locked the car and took her bag with her. Stood in the shop doorway for seconds, inhaling petrol fumes, unable to pull her gaze from the front of the car. It would be fine. Just for a minute. People were looking. Must not stay here.

Things were thrown into the basket. Jars of baby food. Crisps. Fruit. Water. Juice. No real thought to it. Could get more later. She hurried to pay, coins fell on the floor, not neat any more, snatched up and passed, just shoved it all into a carrier bag and left, ignoring the man at the till holding up her change. She had to use the clicker again. It was fine. Baby asleep. No one stopped her. Everything on the back seat. She could drive, pulled out too fast but it was okay, she swerved, and she did not crash.

Once out of sight of the garage she took a side road, then another, doubling back and going in the opposite direction via the B road. They would not expect her to be this clever. And they would not know where she was going.

Not to her house. They would be waiting. Too many of them knew her address. Had it on their papers, printed and clear to read.

Oh no. Not there. She was proud that she'd thought of it as her *house*. Not her *home*, see? Not a home without her baby. They needed a new home. And she'd thought of it while driving, as she touched her baby and remembered the past, long time past, before the painful parts, something happy. It was still in there, part of her, and it would be part of her baby too. So deep inside that They would not know it, not find it printed on their letters, stored in their databases. Only the one in her head. And she wouldn't share that with them any more, she learnt to hide things, because They only used it against you otherwise. Words were twisted and turned back. Painful things got dragged out and pushed at you until your eyes burned and you couldn't forget any more, and if you tried to give that pain back with your hands, to cut it back in to your own flesh to let them know how They were putting broken glass in your heart then They stopped you, and punished you more. No, oh no, all to yourself alone. The only way. Hide the things in your mind, and your baby in the blanket, and nothing could hurt you.

SHE HAD NOT PASSED ANOTHER vehicle in some time. The lanes shrank, hedges untended, branches reaching out to caress the car, tall enough to keep her and the baby in shade. She felt wanted. The good kind of wanted, not the police kind. Once or twice she stopped, unsure of which hemmed-in road to take. In the past they pinned bits of coloured paper on a tree or gate at each crossroads so people knew which way to go. Otherwise many would never had found it, held so far out in the sticks. Some, like this one, were so isolated you couldn't even get taxis there or back. It had always been cars following each other, happy convoys breaking the silence.

She smiled and stroked her baby. Once she was part of the scene, always with others. Sometimes she was one of the earliest, staying in a tent the night before, hanging white sheets from the walls in the DJ room and the chillout room, laughing with the others as they daubed them in luminous paints. Every shape and colour, lines and swirls and smiles. Or she would be part of the group that stayed on afterwards to tidy up, filling binbags with rubbish as the pieces of her head slowly found themselves and gave her personality back. The best parties went on for the whole weekend. A different world. Work forgotten. Family forgotten. Bills forgotten. Baby for–

No!

"I haven't ever forgotten you!" she told the bundle by her side. He was waking. Would be hungry soon. One of the pots had a spoon, it would be easy to feed him. "Whichever flavour you want! Nothing is too much for you. I love you, little one. I won't let anything take you from me this time. Nothing!"

The car had stopped. She didn't remember braking. It was okay. Onwards.

Happy times. Each rave different, but the people often the same. Even in a crowd of two hundred she knew names and faces, and they knew her. There might be fifty from Aberystwyth, then the groups from New Quay, Aberaeron, a minibus from Bristol when it was good DJs, the best dubstep, and hardest drum and bass to shatter your mind like shards of glass. And they did it all, arranging a generator and outside toilet. Some said it was illegal, but it was *theirs*. Not the police's, not the council's, not the Government's. No suits or uniforms, just wedding dresses and wellies; no townie drinking and fighting, just laughing faces and hugs and music; no responsibilities for just a night or two, that was left with her mam. She made a bit of cash helping her friend sell nos balloons: he'd got a big canister of nitrous oxide off the Internet and bought five hundred balloons to fill, cost about £450, sold them for three quid a pop to anyone wanting a light-headed rush. He made about £1,200 in two days, gave her a good cut, and that weekend she loved him, thought they were meant to be, especially when he held her as the sun came up, her legs tired from dancing, jaw tired from smiling. She had loved him all she could, heart and lips and thighs. It wasn't enough.

Even when she was whole, it was never enough.

She recognised the trees here. The leaves were starting to yellow and fall, but the way they grew by the fork in the road, yes, it was her place all right. Only hers now.

Correction: hers and baby's.

The bothies were always in the middle of nowhere. Travellers' rest houses for most of the year, front doors left open, welcoming. No furniture, except the wood-framed beds upstairs that you could chuck a sleeping bag on. Derelict farmhouses surrounded by fields. If that wasn't big enough there might be a ruined barn or room to set up a marquee. Even the travellers cottoned on to it.

The hippies would turn up with a backpack full of bottles of water, sell them for two or three quid and easily make a hundred pounds. And they were respected enough that if they wanted space away from the temporary invaders they'd just go in a bedroom and close the door.

No houses for miles around this bothy. So no neighbours. No police. No ravers even, any more. Not since a girl took too much CK – cocaine mixed with Ketamine, a bad idea for starters – and like a crazy she had stacked MDMA on top. Something unzipped inside her. She died. Very bad. The raves here stopped after her death. Haunted, some said.

It was ideal. Chloe didn't mind ghosts. They were kinder than the living.

She reached the last trail. Slushy mud with a raised grass ridge dividing the ruts. Plant life brushed the underside of the car. No one had been here in a vehicle for some time. No one would be coming, either. She drove slowly, the car bumping and sliding, and she tried to watch out for any big stones hidden by grass which could rip a hole in some vital engine part, could leave it broken and stuck, bogged down in mud forever.

The trail ended at an old metal bar gate. It didn't look padlocked. That was good. She could drive through, and close the gate behind. Another barrier between her and the other world.

As the engine faded to sleep only the sound of their breathing remained, the two of them, alive and free. She unfastened her seatbelt and leaned over baby, tickled him, rubbed her face on his belly, made him laugh while she inhaled that baby smell, love without control, vulnerable but so strong because it made her protective, she'd die for her baby. Whatever she'd once thought, she had been wrong, so wrong not to appreciate it, so wrong to think the worries then were as bad as it could get, and she cried into the blanket while baby pulled at her hair, cried because she loved him so much she wanted to squeeze him hard while gritting her teeth, a squeeze she knew would hurt but that was how much she loved, always so fierce she had to keep a lid on it, a love so hot it scared men away, it could hurt a child, could seem abnormal, even though it was a good thing, this love. If only she could feel it in return. But the love other people talked about or showed was a cold thing by comparison. They'd never felt the searing heat that cleansed all, left skin shiny and thin like wrapping paper on a baby's birthday around a present that was never given.

"I'll die for you," she whispered. "This time, I will."

She wiped her face and checked her phone. It hadn't changed. No signal here. Even if they had worked out who she was they couldn't ring her, try to control her with words. She put the phone back in her jacket pocket. They were alone. In the quiet of a rave long gone, ghost sensations pulling at her as she squeezed her eyes shut, letting one finger stay entwined in her baby's hand, her anchor that would stop her drifting too far.

The drugs hadn't been a bad thing. You could tell by looking at the faces, watching the dancing, giving and receiving the hugs. Some took their own, but she always knew the seller with his little plastic bags all tidy, he'd keep some for her. A lot of people smoked cannabis but she never liked smoking, so went for MDMA as an upper, wrap it in a skin and swallow and you could dance all night, not missing a beat, every bass thump penetrating her, moving her limbs with everyone else's, an electrified group that surrounded her like a hug, wrapped and swallowed her whole. And when morning came with its harsh light and its disappointment and that hollow feeling that the love wasn't real, she had found another answer in the ketamine. K was her tranq, snorted into body and mind to rest them for the second night.

She'd known, vaguely, that ketamine could be dangerous. Seen those passed out unconscious. Knew the ambulance crews around Aberystwyth were used to treating people on K.

She hadn't known what it would be like to disappear down the K-hole herself. Victims can't come out of it easily. An unconscious trip in slow motion where the only escape was to dig your own way out with your broken fingernails. You leave those ones alone. When it first happened to her they joked about Chloe, lost down the C-hole.

They joked, and that made it seem funny, and sometimes she needed to go down that hole just to escape a bit, even in the real world, when her mam wasn't there but baby was, when baby cried and wouldn't stop and nothing you gave him would make him switch the screams for smiles, your hugs meant nothing, your love meant nothing, so that it felt like rejection more times than she could deal with ... then you had to back away. No one could take her love, and it hurt, and sometimes you could snort and see the way out by going within, no matter how dark it was in there. She'd never meant for it to happen. Only her and baby in the flat, should have been safe. Never meant for the fire to start. She'd give anything to go back and –

No! *Fucking no!*

"One minute," she said to her baby. "Mummy needs a minute. To open the gate."

She fumbled out of the car, taking deep breaths, trying to stop the shaking inside, an old engine that couldn't start properly. It was chilly. That helped. She closed the door behind her, mindful of draughts. She would protect this time. No slips, no mistakes. Nothing would separate them ever again. She wouldn't let it.

She mushed through the sodden brown leaves that had formed wet piles, her thin shoes letting the water in so that it squidged cold between her toes. No wedding dress and wellies this time. The gate was tied with thick blue string in a hoop that lifted up over the post. She had to push hard to open it wide enough for the car, as everything growing below tangled it, resisted, had to be broken before the gate could move again the way it was meant to move.

Done. She returned to the car and opened the door.

But it didn't open.

The handle pulled up, and nothing else happened.

She rattled it harder. She pulled in different ways. Locked?

"It's okay, baby," she said, and her voice seemed loud, fast, like her heart, but when she tried the other doors every handle was the same. How? Had the car locked itself? She could see the clicker key inside on the dashboard. It made no sense.

She made the rounds again, surely she had made a mistake, try again, this time it would work. And it didn't.

Now she remembered. Had she heard a noise at the gate, a little click? Or imagined it? Why would the car hate her so much it locked her out?

Baby was wriggling, the blanket falling away. Under the strap. He might fall on the floor. On his head.

Always protect the baby's head!

She banged on the glass with palms sweaty despite the cold.

No! Stay still!

She pulled down her hood, tried to get his attention with her eyes, reassure him she was still there, but he didn't see her, didn't stop wriggling, the noise seemed to make him more upset.

Perhaps a stone.

Nothing at her feet. There must be one! Every field had stones that wanted to trip you! She rushed back and forth, getting her hands wet as she parted the grass, swept leaves aside all slimy, revealing crawlies that twitched out of the light half-seen.

Then: a palm-sized pebble. Not the hefty rock she wanted, but maybe enough.

She was about to bring it down on the driver's side window when her hand froze. A reflection in the glass of a stranger behind her. No, not a stranger. Her hated face, as it was now, all pink and white and shiny down her neck, burns that reached as far as her breast. Numb now, but agony at the time as each nerve exploded and died. Nothing to what was inside, though. She'd crawled through fire for her baby and it hadn't been enough. She must not look at that face. Everyone was right to hate it, even her own mother would spit at it. Yes, that was right. People should look away and puke and know and hate her. She was the first to agree.

She focussed through the glass so it didn't become a mirror, and hit, hard. And again. There would be shards, but as long as they didn't go on baby that was fine. She was no stranger to shards of glass. Her wrists spoke of that. Scars on scars that didn't hurt like what burnt inside. She could see broken glass and not flinch, even though it had let her down, because she was still here, and hospital had patched her up even though she didn't want them to.

But this glass was tough. Her left hand throbbed. Baby was crying now, scared.

She switched hands to the burnt one, that could feel no pain, and hit hard and hard and hard and the best was a crack but Oh! The crying! She could see him, flinching with every breaking blow, it broke her heart, he was scared of her! Oh, that crying, it was too much, she could hear it in her mind, amplified because it added to the crying of the past that returned in sleep, echoing in her head. The impacts pained the one thing she loved, so she dropped the stone, and still he cried, she couldn't stand it, couldn't breathe, so staggered away, saw blood on her hand, it dripped from that horror of a palm and helped her. Squeeze it closed, something that could be fixed. Don't look back. Don't listen. Just enough distance to breathe, through the gate, squelching in mud towards a slope lined with skeletal trees, slipping on the ground but at peace now so that air could enter her lungs again, cold air, and she staggered on with her hands over her face.

When she looked again, she saw the weed-choked building. The front door was closed. That was where it all was, once. But it was silent now, apart from the birds. Now just ghosts. No longer friends, the music, the hugs from strangers. That had all ended the night at home, when she woke to the fire. Everything ended then. She wore her crime and she carried her punishment and she deserved it and could never leave it behind.

Up the hill, using low branches to pull herself on the steepest bits. The fermented smell of decomposing vegetation and damp earth. Everything that lived was just ready to fall and rot. The earth opened up in holes, waiting for us, whether we were ready or not.

It wouldn't work. This life here. The happiness of the past was no more in this field, that house. She had days at most before it would end.

What if she kept walking? On and over the hills, on and on, to her house, not look back, not ever give them a chance to take baby from her? Her secret would wait here. She could return, be with him, like a ghost, like a free woman, like ...

They knew her. They were bound to have worked it out. They would be waiting at her house. She knew what They were like. They would make her tell, eventually. She couldn't lose her baby again.

To not go home then. To go somewhere else. If she left baby they would never find it. It would always be hers.

But then it would be suffering for so long. Baby would know it was her fault. It would leave her. And again, she'd be alone.

She loved it too much for that.

Her foot skidded into a stream – well, more of a trickle – that slipped along beneath the leaves. She scrambled up the other side, near the summit now.

She was thinking clearer as she took in great gasps of autumn air.

She could stay with it. They could be together!

The car contained fuel. There were ways of making sparks. Burns didn't hurt as much as being alone.

At the top she leaned on a sturdy oak to catch her breath, and looked around for the last time. This place was peace, surrounded by autumn colours like fire. Sticks and branches like bonfires waiting to go, leaves ember ashes on the ground. All the world waited for her. Nature understood mothers. Nature understood fierceness. Nature knew you sometimes needed pain to learn. Pain wasn't so bad, but it had to end some time. It wasn't fair if it never ended.

It was getting dark to the east. Day gave up earlier and earlier as the season progressed. Yet the sunset blazed in the other direction, fierce as it fought the dark. It hurt her eyes, made them water like blisters. She knew how it felt. It couldn't win but it refused to give in. Stayed in her sight, lingering, not disgusted with her, not wanting to let it get dark around her like a hole. Each ray reached out. Warm, even where there were no nerves to feel temperature, she imagined it, on her face. A hug. Gone soon, but not an end. It would be back tomorrow. It never surrendered.

She had shielded her baby with her body. She had done her best. The burning love-pain inside let her deal with the burning outside. And she puked up smoke and ash and still crawled out of there. And they took the baby and she felt her face all wet and melting and she retched more and even then didn't care, just wanted them to say her baby wasn't dead, she hadn't killed her baby.

They took it away.

They took it away and she would never see it again.

But it had lived. It had choked on smoke but otherwise not a mark, like a miracle.

And still they took it.

She was hitting herself in the face now, the side that wasn't numb, the side that could feel the wetness of tears that she'd thought dried up long ago. They'd risen again, warm, reaching out like a hug.

Baby hadn't died then. The fire that started while she was lost in her black hole hadn't won, she'd crawled out in time, crawled through, saved her baby. He'd lived then. He should live now. Whatever happened to her didn't matter. They could lock her up, they could call her names, they could put her picture in the paper for everyone to point at, they could turn her mam against her.

Baby loved her. He loved her then, he loved her now. If he never saw her again, he'd still love her. Maybe that was enough.

She took the phone from her pocket. Somehow she knew there would be a signal up here, with the view of the world that still lived all around. This was the view the sun would see tomorrow.

Sometimes the world moved in slow motion. It was like being dead in the grave, and the only escape was to dig your own way out with your broken fingernails. She'd done it before. She wasn't ready to stop yet. Maybe that was love.

She dialled 999 and, between sobs, she asked for the police.

Recalling The Boy

"NOT FOR SWEETS, TOYS, OR computer games."

Dominic read the last line again, grimaced, then crumpled the paper up and threw it across the bedroom. It bounced off the wall and rolled on the floor near his desk.

He was right to be angry.

Uncle Tom had gifted him money – a lot of money. The only good thing he'd done for Dominic since leaving the country. It was potentially great – everyone at school would be jealous – *if* he could spend it.

But he couldn't. Not yet. The document stated that the money was to be kept in trust until Dominic was sixteen (a whole year away!). And even then it was only to be used for university and a limited number of other "worthy" uses – but "not for sweets, toys, or computer games."

The silly phrase made out that he was still a kid.

It just showed how little Uncle Tom had known about Dominic in the last few years. Dominic hadn't seen his uncle since he left for New Zealand when Dominic was eleven. Uncle Tom had written letters, and phoned, but Dominic rarely replied to letters, and found speaking on the phone uncomfortable, until he eventually signalled his mum to say that he wasn't home on the rare occasions that Uncle Tom rang. That became even less frequent in later years. Sometimes just at Christmas.

Christmas. Toys. Sweets. The wording of the gift.

Sweets.

HE USED TO GO SHOPPING with Uncle Tom, to keep him company. Right from when Dominic was a little boy, five or six years old. He remembered sometimes asking for sweets when he saw them, so brightly coloured and tempting. His mum bought them for him – but Uncle Tom never allowed him to have them.

Never!

Uncle Tom would buy him fruit – as much as he wanted – but never sweets. No matter how much Dominic begged or whined or cried.

Restrictions. Always restrictions.

Once, in Woolworths, Dominic had been so angry he had grabbed two handfuls of sweets from the Pick 'n' Mix display, and clenched them tight. He wouldn't let them go, and Uncle Tom had prised his fingers open to remove them, which sent Dominic into a full-blown tantrum in the middle of the shop.

WHAT HAD HAPPENED NEXT? IT was so long ago ... Dominic hunched over on the edge of his bed, thinking.

OH YES. UNCLE TOM HAD paid for the sweets, then given them to a boy outside – a stranger.

Dominic's sweets!

Then Uncle Tom had taken him straight home in silence, and gone shopping without Dominic the next week.

So mean. Dominic had waited by the front door, put his shoes on and tied the laces by himself and everything. He cried when his uncle didn't turn up. Dominic's mum had forgotten to tell him it had been cancelled.

But Uncle Tom had taken him shopping again the week after that. Dominic had expected a lecture, but his uncle didn't mention the incident.

And Dominic hadn't asked for sweets that time.

He did have a juicy plum and three bananas, though.

(How come he'd been able to eat so many bananas as a kid?)

IT WASN'T JUST SWEETS HIS uncle had been bossy about. Toys too. Uncle Tom hadn't let him buy ready-made plastic toys, especially things that required batteries.

"YOU CAN BUY THAT CRAP when you're with your mum and dad."

"But it isn't rubbish!" (He knew he couldn't repeat grown-up words, though didn't understand why.)

"I doubt you'll be saying that when you're bored with it or it falls apart a week from now! Choose something where you have to use your imagination, Dom. It's one of your gifts."

OH YES. HE USED TO be called Dom. "Nephew Dom and Uncle Tom, the reprobates," Uncle Tom used to joke.

As the phrase went through Dominic's mind, it was almost as if a voice echoed around the room for a second, surprising Dominic. The echo even had a hint of the jokey tone his uncle had used.

Jokey, but horribly strict, Dominic reminded himself.

So Dominic used to buy a model or a kit; something that needed building.

LIKE WHEN HE BOUGHT A model aeroplane. Uncle Tom chose one as well, and they spent two days building them together, amid the smudges of paint from their shared plastic pots and the pungent tang of polystyrene cement, while Uncle Tom answered all of Dominic's questions about how planes worked, and why people went to war, and what he should do when he grew up, and if being an astronaut would make him dizzy ...

When the final touch was added – the transfers – Dominic felt so proud, his Airfix 1:72 scale Bristol Bulldog held aloft as he ran to show his dad, making engine noises, and –

– and his dad had told him to be quiet, not to make such a bloody racket –

– and so he hadn't shown him the plane he'd made –

– and Uncle Tom had rested a hand gently on his shoulder and told him the plane was brilliant.

Later they made up a set of rules using dice and had battles between the two planes until Uncle Tom had to go. And Uncle Tom had let him keep both planes.

"Get a few more, and we can make a mobile out of them. It'll look great by your window, so the breeze catches it."

THE CURTAINS BILLOWED OUT IN a sudden gust of wind, making Dominic jump.

Only a breeze.

He got up and moved over to the sash window, which was open slightly.

Today was a cold, bright day. The garden's long grasses were specked with drops of moisture that had frozen overnight, and now twinkled like tiny gems when they caught the light. The kind of day when Uncle Tom would turn up, unexpected, to take him out for a walk.

"YOU CAN'T STAY IN PLAYING video games on a fresh day like this – you've got to stretch your legs, Dom. They're growing and need the exercise, and your eyes need to see the world."

27

And his mum and dad had been arguing again so Dominic was glad to escape with Uncle Tom, instead of feeling confined to his room for fear of getting in the way, and somehow making things worse between his parents.

It was a day like this when Uncle Tom had taken him cycling near the park, all wrapped up with scarf and hat. Uncle Tom had recently got a second-hand bike, which he hardly used (did he buy it just to take Dominic out cycling, because Dominic wasn't confident on his bike and Mum and Dad never seemed to have the time to teach him? No, surely not.). They had pretended to be policemen, using imaginary radios to talk to each other, and Uncle Tom had shouted commands so that they would fall in line, or cycle abreast, or swap positions, accompanied by the flicker flak of frozen leaves under the bike's wheels as they whizzed along, face wind-chilled outside but body warm inside ...

And he had gone on the play park with Dominic and pretended to be a swamp monster while Dominic climbed the frame, avoiding the grabbing hands and screeching like a girl (how old was he then? Eight?) and knowing it was only his uncle, but feeling a thrill of fear anyway as if it was real, and laughing but asking Uncle Tom to stop at the same time, because he was scared, and Uncle Tom had laughed too and lifted him down and put him on a swing and pushed him.

On the way home it had rained, and they rode in big looping circles around the empty car park near the leisure centre, splashing through puddles and making graceful swooshing arcs of spray – until a piece fell off Uncle Tom's old bike. They couldn't work out

28

how it was supposed to go back on, or what it was for, and both laughed until it hurt.

And Mum had told Uncle Tom off when they got back, for having Dominic out for so long and messing up her plans, and she sent Dominic to his room but he hadn't minded at all, because as Uncle Tom walked down the drive, he turned and saw Dominic at his window, and winked a secret wink at him.

YES, HE'D OFTEN COME ON days like this.

Dad had left the next year.

DOMINIC'S MUM HAD CRIED AND said bad words, and Dominic had cried, and things were worse than ever, and he always had to be quiet. Everything in the house whispered "hush" at him: the water tap making a "sssshhhh!" noise when he brushed his teeth; the hiss of the gas in the cooker was a warning just to him; the letters rasping through the letterbox in the morning another "sshh!" just in case he had forgotten overnight.

All that guilt weighed him down, bubbles of fizz gone flat. Until ... yes, until Uncle Tom took him to the annual fair ...

The noise! Bellowing music from the amusements; shouting from the hawkers; screams from those spinning around and upside down. Uncle Tom took him on one of the big rides that bounced high in the air – then, just when you thought it was over, it did the same moves backwards; and Dominic was allowed to scream for so long that the cold air made his throat hurt, and his uncle just encouraged him by telling him the ride had a reputation for breaking, and launching the seats out over Aberystwyth until they crashed down far away, making Dom squeal even louder, but with excitement more than fear...

Uncle Tom had let him pick any five rides to go on, no more, and made him choose carefully, and each seemed all the more precious. Screams on the ghost train, joyful bumps on the dodgems, dizzying whirls on the waltzers. And rather than catching a taxi they walked, spending the money on chips to eat as they talked all the way home about everything and nothing, fingers salty and noses warmed by vinegar steam, and Dominic didn't have any nightmares for the first time in ages.

THERE WERE MANY WALKS IN the dark, chatting, discussing things he couldn't tell his mum, confiding, making up stories, word games ...

Words! See, it wasn't all good. Yet more rules.

SOMETIMES UNCLE TOM HAD MADE Dominic read with him, they took it in turns. Dominic always complained at being forced to read when other things were more fun, and ...

DOMINIC GLANCED AT THE OVERFLOWING bookshelves near his bed, books stacked precariously on the top because every one was full.

Maybe his uncle did have a point. Sometimes.

The top branches of the trees outside swayed gently back and forth, not resisting the wind, but bending in the direction it playfully ruffled them. They moved hypnotically, Dominic couldn't take his eyes off them, they always moved –

THEN UNCLE TOM HAD LEFT him.

SELFISH. FAMILY MEANT NOTHING. UNCLE Tom was only thinking of himself when he fell in love with that woman from New Zealand, and they got married, and Dominic hadn't realised it was a bad thing until Uncle Tom explained that he was going to live in New Zealand with her ...

... AND WHEN DOMINIC FOUND OUT that was the plan he had gone all quiet while Uncle Tom explained and hugged him, and said Dominic could visit if his mum would bring him (though Dominic had known even then that she wouldn't); and Dominic had stayed silent until Uncle Tom was crying and left, and that was the last time he saw him, and he'd heard his mum tell Uncle Tom not to worry, "He'll come round"; but Dominic was so angry it hurt like when he'd trod on glass in the sea, but this was inside; Uncle Tom leaving him just like his dad had, not caring.

Maybe it was Dominic's fault, something wrong with him that drove people away, he was a bad boy and ...

PAIN. IN HIS GUT.

He closed his eyes tightly, fist pushed against the cold glass of the window.

In all these years, this was the first time Dominic had admitted that. It *wasn't* freedom when Uncle Tom left.

Sure, Dominic's mum mostly let him do what he wanted, and she never told him off … never paid much attention at all.

But that wasn't how he really wanted to be treated.

Uncle Tom didn't say no as in "nothing"; he said no as in "do this instead – it is better, or healthier, or more rewarding".

So many memories of his childhood that included his uncle – how could he have buried them for so long? It was as if the anger had been blasted away; rows of Lego walls collapsing, letting memories step out into smarting sunlight, pale and tender from being locked away for years.

Dominic hadn't done anything wrong.

The breeze from the window cooled his cheeks, making the wet tracks feel cold but caressed.

His uncle had left because he *loved* someone, not because he hated Dominic.

It probably hurt Uncle Tom just as much. And Dominic's silence and avoidance over the years must have felt like accusations.

And he still left so much money to Dominic in his will: only to Dominic and Uncle Tom's wife. The two most important people in his life. He'd neglected neither of them.

But it had never been about money. Every memory – it was about time. Time he gave. Time they shared.

And Dominic would have given anything to trade the money for time; even little times on the phone that his anger and pain had stolen from him. Moments like those he had remembered in the last fifteen minutes that felt like they had a lifetime squeezed into them. There would never be a chance for another of those memories to form like a drop of ice. They were gone, melted, his uncle moved on to a place that was further than New Zealand, a place truly beyond reach, with no coming back.

Dominic took the crumpled ball of paper and unfolded it, smoothing it gently with the palm of his hand.

"Not for sweets, toys, or computer games."

He wiped his eyes with the back of his hand, and let out a half-laugh, half-sob.

Dominic could almost imagine the gentle pressure of a loving hand on his shoulder.

SenSor OS

YOUR OPERATING SYSTEM HAS BEEN updated to SenSorSoft OpenDoors 11! Features:

No more low-quality free software! All software now has to be purchased and installed from the inbuilt AppStore, a selection of APProved quality tools, for your convenience!

No more update hassles! This software-as-a-service will receive automatic updates without you needing to consent to them, for your convenience. The previous versions of your OS are no longer supported (for security reasons), and activation requests will be denied.

Your licences have been transferred and will be periodically verified while online: any software for which the licence is absent, void, expired, or deprecated, will be removed for your convenience. Software which is not available in the AppStore will be quarantined.

All your office software has been replaced with the FREE online 247FreedomSuite (ad-supported). This will enable you to remain compliant with all possible legislation: for your convenience!

The new software will personalise itself to you! Our Sensei tool genuine intelligence services will monitor everything so that tools can be personalised. We guarantee your privacy!*

Note: you must be permanently online for full functionality of the tools and services. Services and software can be improved (changed) or removed at any time, without notification. Offline mode not guaranteed.

Please tick the box to show that you agree to all the legally binding TERMS & CONDITIONS** (details available in the support section of our website, broken into 457 pages and sections for your convenience).

*Data may be stored and utilised and shared by us and our trusted partners so as to improve services and personalise your experience, for your convenience.

**You grant to SenSorSoft a worldwide and royalty-free intellectual property license to use Your Content, for example, to make copies of, retain, transmit, reformat, display, monetise, and distribute via communication tools Your Content on the Services.

THERE WAS NO OPTION BUT to click "I agree".

She'd known that the latest versions of the operating system were an enforced upgrade, and that previous versions would be deactivated, but it still smarted to see this message filling the screen when she plonked down her coffee cup and turned on the laptop today. She'd spent years setting it up the way she wanted. But you had to move with the times. The alternative commercial operating systems had switched to this same model a year ago. The only other option was Linux, but the new DeoldoCheck DRM methods big companies now used meant all the games and software she'd bought would fail to run on any open system. She'd complained online about the forced changes but the heads of global software companies paid no attention – she was just another angry amoeba caught in their ecosystem. It was no surprise when SenSorSoft didn't even have a consistent naming policy. Their releases of OpenDoors had gone from version RC, to 2.1, to ME, to U, to 94, to 360, to One, to We, to 9, to 10.3. Best to make a brave face of it.

FIVE HOURS AND A NUMBER of hot drinks later.

It seemed she'd "activated successfully" (which involved rebooting the router and entering all her personal details into a profile screen and accepting further terms and conditions). She wasn't allowed to use her old username so created a new one. She still didn't know how to find or browse the hard drive, which had been "virtualised for convenience". It seemed that the only way to find things was to type them into a search box that appeared if you moved the mouse pointer to the top left, then the bottom right of the screen. You could also say the name of the program you wanted, but the operating system AI, Susie, had a problem with Scottish accents. Its only voice options were a variety of US dialects. She'd tried saying "Open word processor," "I want to type a letter," and "Just give me something to fuckin write with!" but it simply kept loading a calculator, and closing it down took three clicks and a weird swipe. She stuck to typing, and closed the window that popped up every ten minutes reminding her that the computer now had voice control. She clicked more angrily each time. The left mouse button had started to make a spronging noise.

Still: the grey void of a blank page faced her, with its blinking cursor of optimism. She had so many ideas for this new novel. There had been little success with her books so far, but *this one* could be it. She felt it in her bones. The one that would get her noticed. Reviews, adoring fans, maybe even royalties. Oh, she needed the money. It was make-or-break, and she'd break hard.

> *The door opened with a creak. McWerter held his breath, afraid that the man he'd come to kill would hear the betraying noise, would draw his gun and fire first ... but no. Silence. He slipped into the bookshop with the ease of a professional killer. The place was an Aladdin's cave of*

One of the words faded from the screen and a message popped up.

"Rights database checked: [Aladdin] is a trademark of the Disney Corporation."

It now read "an cave of".

What the fuck?

She typed "Aladdin" again, but the word was erased immediately as soon as she pressed the final letter. Same popup, though it had a note that she'd received a second copyright warning. Whatever. Fix it for now, try to disable the options later. (It had to be an option, right?)

Okay. A what cave? She leaned back, trying to think of an alternative.

A few minutes on and she gave up. The flow was broken. Pish.

Three windows had piled up reminding her about new features. She closed them all.

Move ahead. Think about the next scene. Get back into the mood. All she had to do was start. Once she imagined it, she'd fall into the page, and the words would come. She sipped more black coffee. The bitterly energising smell of it permeated her office like a noir detective's cigarette smoke. Okay, it needed some interpersonal tension. Dialogue to spark conflict.

"Is that a pistol in yer pocket or are ye just pleased ta see me?" Betty asked.

McWerter had expected an exotic femme fatale dressed in red, but coffee-shop Betty looked nothing like how she'd sounded on the phone. A 60-year-old Glaswegian fishwife whose tights bagged around the ankles. When no reply came to his dry mouth she held up her cigarette.

"Well, at least stop glowerin and light a lady's fag."

McWerter reached

Another word faded: this time the message that popped up said:

"[Fag] removed: offensive."

This was ridiculous. She angrily bashed out "FUCK YOU YOU FANNY DICK SHIT COMPUTER!!!!!!"

As expected, words faded. Though not all of them. She was left with:

"YOU YOU FANNY COMPUTER!!!!!!"

Och, must be an American database.

SHE SET ASIDE THE NOVEL. She would come back to it when her hand stopped clenching into a fist. Maybe she just needed to get into the flow via another project.

Her desk did not face the window, since a view would be too distracting when she had to get four thousand words down a day. Instead she let her gaze wander. Overlapping rings of coffee stains where her spillages marked daily progress in a pattern of Os. A fireplace that she couldn't use even on shivery days because it would smoke her out (note to self, must get that chimney swept). Framed photos of family and friends, the alive and the dead.

Her life diary! Perhaps one day she'd be famous enough to repurpose it as an autobiography, but for now it was just something to keep her sane. So much of our past is lost, left to the soft mercies of decaying synapses. Pictures miss out more than they capture. But *words* ... ah. That can be the whole picture. The smells, the sounds, the thoughts, the feelings. This was why writing was so important. It captures and encodes experience and emotion, enables it to live on beyond the person; inefficient organic storage and retrieval replaced with perfect silicon. Life was nothing without memories. The beautiful, the ugly; the soothing, the painful. It is what we are. What we pass on to the world. They should be saved, and deserved the time to do it, to find the perfect words and the perfect order so that we do not go gently into that black hole.

> *I remember my first dog. The boys wouldn't let me play football, but I didn't need them. I needed the puppy sat in the pet shop window, as unloved as I was. And I'd go in and stroke her, and keep asking the shop keeper how much she cost. She was a healthy*

"[Bitch] removed: offensive."

> *The other girl knew I was watching. It must have been a game to her. She was beautiful. I was a scrawny teenager with glasses and no friends, who sat on her window ledge playing Fighting Fantasy books. Until the day when things changed. When I saw her saunter past the house, provokingly slow; the way she avoided looking up at my window; I snapped. I ran out of the house, grabbing something on the way, and I followed her. And she was surprised as she turned to find me holding out a juicy*

"Rights database checked: [apple] is a trademark of Apple Computers."

> *A year later. My heart races as I hand her the letter. But I will not run. Not this time. She takes it from my hand*

*without smiling. I knew I was a fool. Because all it said
was:*

and your fruit

"[P.S. I love you] removed: copyrighted song lyrics."

This was ridiculous. Maybe if she was really careful about what she typed, tried to second-guess problem words for now, think of ways to work around it, to –

Awa an shite, what was she thinking! She was the one in charge. She wouldn't be outwitted by a corporate bawbag. What would she end up with? The blandest focus-grouped prose that was so safe it would send any reader to sleep; an arse wiped clean "for her convenience".

First she tried to find a setting to turn off the Wi-Fi on the laptop. Down nine layers of nested menus that circled back to the start, but no disable option. Right. The sleekit bastard. She stomped downstairs and turned off the router at the plug socket.

"Take that and bile yer heed, ya fuckin walloper!"

Back upstairs to be greeted with:

"Error. Internet connectivity is missing or slow. Cloud functionality impaired."

She clicked okay, but the message reappeared seconds later. Click click click, it was like whack-a-mole at the funfair, a new one blinked into existence as fast as she could crack their skulls. For fuck's sake, how long would this take?

Back downstairs, router back on. It was only a temporary retreat. She wouldn't be beat by this pissfartin machine.

"Internet connectivity restored. Personal files transferred to your free Skycloud Service and converted to a new format. Would you like to access your new .wpdx documents?"

"Aye, ah would!" she shouted.

"Sorry, I don't understand, please repeat that," said the nasal voice from her speakers.

She clicked "Okay". It was important to at least make sure she had backups of her novels. They were backups, right? That's what it meant? Just because she couldn't find her files on the hard drive, they must be there somewhere. Maybe this was only her old notes that had been uploaded.

A list of her previous works appeared. Each one had a mysterious exclamation mark in a triangle. She clicked on the exclamation mark next to the document at the top of the list – her first book, a collection of short stories that she hoped to update later in the year. Various messages scrolled down the screen.

Mr the quiet man missed her.

"[Adcock] removed: contains offensive word."

So the secret was hidden behind the statue of !

"[Isis] removed: unsanctioned name for terrorist organisation."

Ah loved it when ma mam read Winnie The h to me.

"[Poo] removed: offensive."

Ancient Greek wrestlers would enter naked and oiled, but were only held every four years.

"Unlicensed use of [the Olympics]: not allowed within a radius of fifty miles of the games."

The list went on: removed as possible plagiarism; removed as dangerous advice according to health and safety guidelines; removed as illegal advice that might facilitate circumventing DRM under the updated US DMCA Act.

"But ah live in Dundee, ya radge wee shite!" she yelled at the screen.

"Sorry, I don't understand you, please repeat yourself," it replied.

A whole scene set in a supermarket had been deleted for being "potentially negative" concerning a SenSorSoft trade partner; another was disallowed because it went against the Terms and Conditions she'd apparently agreed to once while doing an online order for a new phone.

She turned the computer off at the plug before putting her fist through the screen. "Get tae fuck, arsepiece!" So much for fuckin convenience.

SHE TOOK A DEEP BREATH and rebooted. She'd spent the last hour cursing and hitting the Laphroaig bottle that had been intended as a treat for Christmas, wrapping her computer-monitor-sliced knuckles in a bandage, and opening the window to waft away the smell of singed electronics. Then she dug out her old external monitor and a backup drive. Whatever was happening to the files on the laptop, and wherever they really were, she had further copies here. She'd been careful about backups after reading I.T. horror stories.

It took over ten minutes to get back to a logon screen, following a variety of warnings about unexpected errors, potentially corrupted files, and always leaving the computer turned on by following correct standby procedures rather than ever turning it off fully "and missing vital updates". The delay and messages seemed to be a punishment, and she was suitably chastised by the time she was allowed access to the desktop again.

The external drive was connected. A list of files and folders magically appeared as expected. She double-clicked on the first backup file.

"Permission denied. Security settings restrict access to user *sodoff* and Administrator *PC Workgroup231*. Please contact your administrator if you require assistance."

And the next file. And the next.

You had to move with the times.

She didn't stop kicking until the sparking plastic pieces were crushed and scattered all across the office.

The 6.30 Hole

October 1999

PAUL TINKLED A TEASPOON IN his empty cup while Jen finished her biscuit. She didn't seem to be paying any attention to the irritating sound as she stared vacantly at the clouds outside. The only other noise was the slosh of traffic on the wet main road two stories below the window of their flat. It had recently stopped raining but was still grey and overcast.

"Huh. Looks like a walk in the woods is out. It'll be far too muddy," Paul said, with slightly too much volume.

"Yes."

He picked at bobbly bits on his jumper.

After a while she glanced at him and said, "It's so gloomy. I'm sure autumns never used to be this grey."

He stared at her. "Weather can't be gloomy. Only people."

"I guess so." She frowned and looked out of the window again.

He had enjoyed the meal, but as usual he hated the bit afterwards, before they left the table to go and do some reading. Time slowed down, and they both just stared at the same view out of the same window. Sometimes it wasn't so bad, especially when it was sunny, or the sunset was particularly beautiful, but on nights like tonight it dragged. To rush away from the table immediately would seem like retreat, so he sat it out. She looked out of the window, sometimes stroking her blonde fringe away from her eyes.

"What are you thinking, Jen?"

"Nothing much."

"But you must be thinking something!" he insisted.

"I'm just watching that woman walking down the road. She's struggling with two kids at her sides, and a baby in her arms."

"She shouldn't have had three kids then."

Jen didn't bother to reply. After a while, once the right amount of time had elapsed, he got up and left the kitchen. She finally looked away from the window and picked up the teaspoon he had been fiddling with, turning it slowly. Then she dropped it back into the cup and got up too.

November

THEY WERE FINISHING OFF A pasta dish he'd made. It had been flavourless and bland. Needed something. Salt. Maybe chilli. As

46

soon as the cutlery went down, she looked out of the window again.

"Jen!"

"What?"

"Look at me."

She turned from the window, an eyebrow raised.

"Don't you think it's like a morgue in here sometimes?"

She laughed unexpectedly, then replied, "Sometimes. Not all the time. I only notice it around now."

"Exactly! After we've had a meal and are both sat here. It feels like I'm in a pub and everyone's in a bad mood, and no one has had their first drink yet. And we're like this most nights." He was getting excited. He'd wanted to discuss this for some time.

"Maybe," she said. "Words aren't always needed."

"But it isn't that they aren't necessary, it feels like there *are* no words. No, that's not quite right ..." He lost his train of thought, so tried a different approach. "Anyway, we weren't always so quiet."

"It's just the way couples get eventually, Paul. My parents were the same."

"But they don't count as normal."

"That's not fair!" She seemed hurt.

"Sorry. But why haven't we discussed this before?"

"Why should we?"

"Don't be so apathetic. We used to discuss everything."

"Did we? I'm not so sure."

"I am."

The conversation wasn't going the way he had imagined. His plan had been that they'd discuss their problem and find some answer, some reason why 6.30 p.m. was such a miserable time of day. He often thought about it. But the chance was slipping away, her face losing animation – he guessed she would look out of the window again soon. Maybe he shouldn't have said anything about her parents. She seemed more sensitive nowadays.

"Look, I just wanted to know if everything was okay."

She sighed. "Never mind. Everything's fine. Come on, let's sort out the bills."

She got up and shuffled into the living room in her ridiculous too-big monster-feet slippers. She used to go barefoot around the house.

Late November

"JEN, LET'S GET A HI-FI."

She put down her fork, and the dark green sprout that had been halfway to her open mouth rolled off it.

"Why? Neither of us are into music."

"Maybe we should be. I've been thinking –"

"Uh-oh."

"Seriously, I was trying to work out what we lacked."

"Not *that* again ... We don't *lack* anything. Give it a rest, Paul. You're like a terrier, shake shake shake until you've worried something to rags." She resumed eating.

"Yes, *that* again. I think we do lack something. And I think it's music, and sound. No TV, no radio, no hi-fi. Just the endless drone of traffic outside. Remember when we had a meal with Cleo and Pol before we went to the pictures? They had that classical stuff playing, very stylish, wine and everything. And when we stayed with my brother he always had the latest albums on, and everyone was talking."

"Everyone was shouting, more like. You couldn't hear the person next to you."

"It wasn't that bad. Anyway, I reckon it would make the place more cosy. We could get a few different CDs and try it out. Kill the silence."

"Neither of us like noise."

"Music isn't noise."

"Some of it is."

"We wouldn't buy that type."

"It's an expensive thing just to try out."

"But we can afford it! We haven't treated ourselves for ages. And we could always sell it if it turns out to be rubbish."

She put her forefingers together under her chin and thought for a few seconds before resting her hands back on the table.

"Okay. It's Saturday tomorrow. We'll get one then, when we do the shopping."

He grinned, surprised by how agreeable she was. He had planned this suggestion for a while – chewing things over was a habit of his – and she'd always resisted much more in his imagination. He rested his right hand on her left wrist, and smiled into her beautiful, dark brown eyes. So deep. She smiled back, and a weight fell from him, leaving euphoric lightness as if they'd come through a dark cloud and now the sun shone. The back of his mind said it was silly to be so excited about buying some electronics, that he was as much of a gullible consumer as the next person if he bought into the "purchase this and be happy" ideology. But he ignored that voice, and turned to his mashed potatoes.

Early December

"GRUB'S UP!" SHOUTED JEN, LAYING the table.

Paul threw his magazine down, rushed over to the stereo, and turned it on. Then he chose the random play option for the CD. Burning Down The House by Talking Heads came on, and he smiled with satisfaction. The stereo was silver and blue, a mini sound system, and had all sorts of options they hadn't even tried yet. It had cost them a hundred quid at Dixons a couple of weeks ago, and was switched on at various times of the day – the most important being 6 p.m., when dinner was served. They only had three CDs, chosen pretty much at random. They had asked the Mancunian guy in Woolworths for three CDs by various bands, saying they didn't know much about the music scene. He had given them a funny look then just pointed them unhelpfully at the "3 for £15" section. As well as The Best Of Talking Heads they had bought Radiohead's OK Computer and Daft Punk's Homework. Paul and Jennifer didn't like the third album, it was too silly and made them feel like they were missing the joke, but the Radiohead album had some nice music, and Talking Heads made them want to dance.

Paul did a comical shoulder-shaking move as he approached the table, and Jennifer grinned as she served steaming aromatic sauce over their spaghetti, and poured them a glass of wine each – a treat they'd begun to indulge in during the last fortnight. They sat and tucked in, eating hungrily, sipping wine, and grabbing crusty bread or spoonfuls of salad to go with the main dish.

"Mmmm, this is gorgeous, Jen."

"Glad you like it, it's easy to make. Just tomatoes, garlic, olives, houmous, basil. A guy in work passed it on to me."

"You'll have to tell him how much we love it. Can you hand me the bread basket and marge?" He spoke with his mouth full, "continental style", and she dripped sauce onto her blouse and just shrugged, which made them both laugh.

They finished the main course and had melon for dessert. The album continued to play – Psycho Killer made them grin even more, as they sang the "Fa-fa-fah fah, fa-fa-fah fah" bit together. They had both finished eating, but not talking: the conversation went on as they planned next year's summer holiday, and discussed the renovation of the old theatre, and how Cleo and Pol were splitting up. The flat seemed so alive! Neither of them wanted to leave the table; it was the cosiest they'd been for some time.

"Any wine left?" Paul asked.

Jennifer checked the bottle and shook her head. "We've finished it again. Or rather you have, you alcoholic! I never knew you could put it away so easily."

"What do you mean? You've had more than me, you cheeky sod!"

She leaned over and kissed him.

"What was that for?" he asked.

"I don't know, I felt like it. There doesn't have to be a reason for everything we do. And maybe there's more where that came from ..."

Her palm rested on his knee under the table, which created pleasant sensations to go along with the merry feeling of slight intoxication.

"Oh yeah? Like what?"

Jennifer took his hand, leading him out of the kitchen, through the living room and into the bedroom, the dirty dishes left for later.

December Still

"I'M PUTTING IT OUT NOW," said Paul, arranging the last of the cutlery on the table.

Jennifer walked over to the stereo and pressed random play. Karma Police by Radiohead came on, and she sighed, perhaps with satisfaction. They'd bought more albums recently, but she didn't feel like those tonight.

She waited at the table as Paul laid out plates of garlic bread, chilli and salad. He held up the bottle of wine but she shook her head, so he poured himself a glass and put the rest back in the fridge. Then he sat down and began to eat.

They didn't speak much during the meal, and both finished before 6.30 p.m. Jennifer looked out of the window at the orange-lit street, watching the lights of the cars moving off into the darkness. Paul stared at her, his eyes glistening as if he had just put his contact lenses in.

"What did you think of the meal?" he asked.

"It was nice. I like garlic bread."

Silence.

"Is that all you've got to say, Jen?"

"What do you want me to say?"

"Nothing."

Pause.

"Too cold for a walk tonight," he said, playing with his knife, wiping crumbs from the sharp blade.

"Yes. Far too cold. It's going to frost up." She pulled her cardigan tighter around her shoulders as if the room had suddenly got colder too.

He finished off his wine and put the knife down. It was at least thirty seconds before he spoke.

"Jen!"

"What?"

"What's going on? Look at me please!" The last word sounded like begging. She glanced at him, her eyes dark and shaded, but shining.

"It's happening again, Jen. I don't know what to do. I hate this ... this silence between us. There are no words. Nothing to say. Why?"

Subterranean Homesick Alien had begun to play, its haunting notes echoing around the kitchen.

"I don't know, Paul. I really don't."

"I thought everything was going to work."

Pause.

"But I don't feel like listening to music any more, Jen."

Pause.

"I'm hurting," he said softly.

They looked away from each other. He rubbed his eyes but she still didn't reply. The door banged behind him as he exited the kitchen, making her flinch. Only then did she look away from the window, and rest her face in her hands.

December End

PAUL LOOKED OUT OF THE window for the last time. Jennifer was out, perhaps on purpose. He'd packed the few possessions that he hadn't taken with him the night before. This was the last time he would see that view of the road below.

A pained grimace crossed his face for a second.

"I hate this view!" He spoke to the empty room, then laughed, without humour. "I've always hated it!"

Two nights ago he had finally realised why they didn't talk. The music was like the cementing-over of an underground river that had long ago run dry, unnoticed. From the surface all seems solid, but beneath isn't the firm ground you expect.

He picked up his suitcase and walked out.

Below The Surface

1 hour

WINSTON COLLAPSED ON HIS BACK and the wet sand crunched to accommodate him. His head was heavy, dreads drenched with sea water. Lying down also meant the cutting wind and rain had less to get hold of, but the view of the black sky sent ice into his bones, and the shivering started again.

"I thought you'd never stop coughing up water," he said, turning his head to where she lay. She was barely visible in the near-dark, a vague ghostly shape.

She didn't answer, still too busy crying. She hadn't moved either, hadn't crawled away from the salt-water vomit she'd been spewing since he dragged her from the sea. He'd done some of that too. Sea water formed acid in the gut. His throat still burned, scratchy and raw.

Back up at the cloud-filled sky while rain pummelled down. She was in shock. Give her time. He was grateful to be alive.

2 hours

THEY HAD TO CLIMB HIGHER. It was hard to gauge how big the island was in the darkness, but he could tell it was shrinking as the tide rose. The level sand they'd first crawled onto was already swallowed up under waves. At waist depth they'd be powerful enough to suck you back from the land, reclaim you for the sea you thought you'd escaped.

Storm clouds churned, grey shreds glowing when they crossed the moon, impenetrable mass elsewhere. Beyond the sand a rocky area erupted from the earth. Higher ground. Sharp edges cut into his hands and knees, which slipped into freezing pools of unknown depth, where slick and fleshy masses flinched.

He had to watch her as they scrambled up. Make sure she didn't drop behind, or give in. It was exhausting, since the rain continued to lash down from the hurricane that had struck.

They reached the highest point. It was encrusted with barnacles. That wasn't a good sign. He didn't say anything. Occasional lightning flashes deep within the clouds reflected off the rising waters, which already encroached on the low rocks. Thunder followed each brief illumination almost immediately, a body-penetrating peal of doom telling them they were in the heart of the storm, and they were tiny.

His stomach clenched when he remembered the waves out at sea. He hadn't known they could be so high. The top-heavy cruise ship that had seemed so large when he joined the crew, even though it was comparatively small compared to normal ocean liners, had been smashed around like a toy. When he'd paused on the deck, and seen one of the waves rearing up, that massed wall of drowning destruction, something had tipped in the world, not just the surface but the madness of it, the insignificance of the ship, of the crew, the passengers. He'd clung to the rail for his life as the ship rode the monstrous swell at a gut-wrenchingly steep angle, and had refused to look out at the waves again. Just tried to find his way to someone senior, to find out what he should do, down claustrophobic corridors that tilted nightmarishly and slammed him against the walls until he thought his shoulder was broken.

If one of those sky-reaching waves hit the island now it would wash over them, sweeping the pitiful bit of land clean in seconds.

3 hours

NO HUGE WAVE, BUT THE waters continued to rise. Their small rocky plateau was only inches above sea level now. A sinking liferaft made of stone. Larger waves washed over the edge, wetting his feet all over again, while the buffeting wind threatened to throw them into the sea.

He put his arm around her, kept her close to the highest point, and told himself he did it for her, even though he knew it was really for him, because after all they'd been through the rising cold blackness was enough to make anyone go mad. Perhaps it would have been better to drown with the ship. A few minutes of horror rather than a drawn-out torment in the dark.

4 hours

THEY SQUATTED, AND THEIR LEGS and waists were below the surface of the sea. *Everything* was below the surface of the sea. Only water, all around, undulating with horrible movement, home to mystery, while pelting rain soaked them from above as well.

When the clouds parted to reveal the moon, temporarily banishing the pitch dark, it was worse. It felt like he floated. If not for the slippery rock below him his mind could drift away completely.

The water now came up to his chest, her neck. Really they should stand, but when he'd tried it was dizzying, not seeing your feet; and it was so slippery that he was on the edge of falling, plunging off the rocky ledge into deeper water. So he'd squatted again and held her close. She muttered in a language he couldn't place. It didn't feel like anything remained in her except those alien words and residual heat. A body, not a person.

His teeth chattered, and his legs went numb with the iciness. He pissed himself, a few seconds of warmth before that, too, washed away.

Everything solid was being taken. He wondered if anyone had ever felt so alone.

5 hours

THE STONE THEY SAT ON was still under water, but the sea had receded. His knees broke the surface. The wind and rain abated. The constant pushing and pulling of the waves, that made it hard to keep his bottom on the rock, had also faded.

He asked her if she was alive and she didn't answer, and he had the premonition that he embraced a corpse. His arm was too stiff and locked in place from the firm hold to loosen it easily. Cracking in the joints as he tried. Then she turned her head slightly and her eyes were open. He left his arm there.

6 hours

SAT ON DAMP ROCK. THE waters receded quickly now, revealing craggy stone dotted with rock pools, and smooth white sand beyond and lower down. Light spread on the horizon, dawn approaching, welcome orange pushing away the darkness. The sky cleared as the storm passed, refreshing sea breeze replaced the howling winds, breaking up clouds.

Black hair hung over her face as she gazed down. When he spoke to her she looked at him, but something was missing from her eyes, as if she wasn't fully awake. He guessed at Japanese, but perhaps Filipino was more likely here. She showed no signs of understanding, but he talked anyway, because it helped hide his hollowness from her, helped him avoid falling into it, kept him strong on the outside.

They'd survived, but he couldn't stop shaking.

7 hours

IN THE DAYLIGHT IT WAS easy to see the scope of the island, if you could really call it that when it got fully submerged. At one end was the dark rocky protrusion that had saved their lives. Not separate rocks piled up, but one mass of sharp edges. It looked bubbled in places. Maybe it was volcanic. About twenty metres wide at the base; by the time you scrambled up the rough sides to the highest points it was only a few metres across.

On one side of that outcrop was the superfine shifting white sand that ran in an elongated line. From the sky it must have resembled one of those cuttlefish bones you wedged between the bars of a budgie's cage. Below the water's surface the sand sloped gently away. At low tide the beach was around twenty metres wide, and a hundred metres long. Nothing grew on it. A treeless paradise amidst the azure sea and holiday-brochure skies.

The other side of the rocky uprising was just a steep sub-sea drop into deep dark.

The island held no fresh water. Stupid, but he'd tasted the liquid in the rock pools anyway. Like warm sweat with a bitter tang. You can't live long without water, but they would eventually be found. They just had to hold out until then.

They walked about on the sandy area. His joints ached, but despite the pain it was good to be moving. He flapped his arms against his body, savouring tingling sensations in the extremities. She stood gazing out to sea. Looking for something.

The water left a few items as it receded. He took his soaking socks and trainers off and waded through the crystal-clear blueness. A dead fish, partially decayed. A plastic bag, empty. A small hardshell suitcase that floated. He pulled it up the sand and opened it eagerly. It had stayed watertight. Inside were women's clothes, neatly packed. Sunglasses. A bag of toiletries. But no food or water. His mouth was salty and parched.

He showed the suitcase to her, and she nodded, which was the most she'd communicated. She was much shorter than him. The waters of the night must have been even more terrifying for her as it reached her neck, not knowing when it would stop rising. And yet she hadn't shown fear. Only tears. He suspected they weren't tears for herself.

There had been another man in their life raft. Australian. It can't have been him she mourned, they hadn't seemed to recognise each other. Just three strangers being tossed into each other's arms as every wave lifted them up with a dreadful sense of vertigo, and the knowledge that what goes up must go down. And yet it stayed afloat for a long time, most of the night, blown in spinning circles across the tempestuous surface. Then it finally tipped. No idea what happened to the Australian. No, she was looking for something else.

Further out. Something big and red. At first he wondered if it was a life raft, deflated, but then decided it seemed more like a plastic barrel. He took off his jeans, tried wading out even further but it kept getting deeper until the under-foot sandy surface dropped off a shelf. The water near that darkness was icy cold. He couldn't face swimming out over that drop. Not yet, with the terrors of last night so close.

If only the life raft reappeared. He'd risk swimming out for *that*. A shelter. Something to sit in when the water rose. And there had been a box of supplies in it. Food and water and flares. He wished he'd been able to grab a few of those items before it tipped them into the sea and forced them to scramble up the beach. All gone.

He sank onto the drying sand. Made from millions of pieces of stone and shell, and still it didn't feel solid.

8 hours

SHE SAT BY THE EDGE of the water, clutching her knees, wearing a pleated skirt and a white sleeveless blouse with a collar that resembled giant flower petals. He'd persuaded her to take her shoes off and let them dry out. Her feet seemed tiny and pale next to his large brown ones.

"Do you speak *any* English?" he asked.

"Boy," she said, looking up at him with her dark eyes that he was sure would be tear-filled if she had any left. "Little boy." She gazed out at the sea again, dry amidst the wet.

It wasn't really an answer to his question, but at the same time, it was.

9 hours

SHE STARED OUT AT SEA, and he stole more glances at her. Maybe she *was* familiar to him after all. Winston could have glimpsed her on the ship. There were so many passengers. But now he'd seen her up close so much, he remembered her – with a small boy. Two of them. A happy-looking boy, and she stood behind him and held his shoulders.

Or perhaps he imagined it, creating false memories as a distraction. The colours in that vision were too bright, the people too still, like a photograph.

She shuddered and pointed. Something heavy and brightly coloured tumbled in the breakers as if they played with it. He waded out in his boxers.

It was a body. A man. Swollen. Accusing blank eyes open, skin puffy and pale. One of the crew, still with his jacket on. Winston didn't recognise him – maybe it was catering team, hospitality. Nearly as many staff as passengers, he couldn't know all his colleagues.

He searched the man's pockets. In one he found a half-eaten packet of cough drops. The sodden wrappers were peeling off each sweet which crumbled with salt water, but he popped one in his mouth and sucked. After the salt came the sweetness, and he almost cried as saliva moistened his mouth. Sugar for energy. He couldn't do anything for the man but took his jacket and returned to the woman, dropping the jacket on the sand and holding out the sweets as he stood shivering in the breeze.

She shook her head but he said "Please" and persuaded her to take one, to put it in her mouth. They had to keep their energy up until rescuers came.

10 hours

ANOTHER BULKY SHAPE ROLLED IN the waves. He'd given up hoping it was just a bundle of clothes. Why hadn't these people all got to the life rafts? Maybe for the same reason he nearly didn't make it to one before the ship sank: the chaos and the tilting boat, blocked routes, darkness, alarms and panic, trampled bodies and screaming.

He couldn't leave this one, though. Smaller than the others.

He glanced at her but she hadn't noticed, she was turning their clothes over as they dried under the baking Pacific sun. How could the sky be so clear and blue so soon after the hurricane? Nature was beyond comprehension.

He was putting it off. Who wanted to see the undulating corpse of a child? If it was, he didn't know if he'd tell her.

He waded out, feet sinking into the sand. As he got closer he could see something was wrong. The head was too big.

Every step nearer was an effort, pushing through water that now reached his waist, aware that he approached the cold drop off, the black abyss that marked the end of solid ground. He wanted to close his eyes and splash back to the island, but this could be important.

Not a boy. A man. Passenger. Patterned shirt. Then it made sense.

His legs were missing. Torn off. It was difficult to examine in the rippling water, and Winston didn't want the body to wash against his legs – it was hard enough holding back sick – but bite marks pierced the remaining thigh, where a chunk had been torn

64

away. Swollen and bloodless punctures. The same on the torso, which was partially eaten. Large triangular holes. He'd seen them in pictures. He backed out of the deep water so fast that he fell over the first time, face submerging and vision obscured, sound muffled. He came up spluttering and darting panicky eyes around, watching for dark shapes below the surface.

11 hours

THE TIDE ROSE AGAIN, QUICKLY swallowing up the flat beach and forcing them into a smaller dry area.

He kept scanning the skies, but it was so hard to see anything against the insane brightness, especially in the eye-watering sun's direction.

A short while ago there had been a speck up there. Whether it was a bird, a plane, or a helicopter, it was too small and distant to tell. Even if it was closer they had no flares, nothing to light a fire with, no way of laying out a sign. He'd give anything to be back home on Maho Beach, risking a roaring jet blast in the face as planes descended to Princess Juliana Airport, flying so low you could almost jump and hit the jet with a stick to get the pilot's attention.

Rescue would arrive soon. They must be combing the area in widening rings. This wasn't a teeny sailer, or a skeleton-crewed cargo ship that had gone down. It was a packed cruise ship, the kind of thing that would be all over the news, headlines selling papers across the Asia-Pacific region and beyond.

Over-packed, it now seemed, especially the newer above-deck cabins after the operator tarted up the public areas.

Winston's job was supposed to be entertainments, playing backing music for the evening events. At the start it was a laid-back gig, with time off when he found himself in demand from rich white women who'd happily forego day trips in port so they could pretend they were *daring* and *desired* and *exotic*. But when a stomach bug hit the crew and passengers he had to cover other jobs and do extra shifts, and it topped out at more than a seventy-five hour week.

And then something went badly wrong while a groaning proportion of those on board spent their time shitting beans. Maybe there was a navigation problem. An issue with the reports. With the failsafes. Maybe a freak no one could have predicted. The ship wasn't owned by a big operator, but one on the margins. Over the years the boat had been handed around the large cruise companies, refitted numerous times. One of the crew let slip that the ship had fifteen different names behind it.

Maybe lots of things went wrong at once. Whatever. When the storm hit they were too far out to do anything but weather it and call for help. Help didn't come in time. People turned to the crew, not realising Winston and those like him were just as clueless. He'd not had any decent training, and the emergency drill was based around calmness, flat sea, good lighting, and orderly behaviour: not tipping floors, injuries, stampeding, lights failing. That was when things descended into dog-eat-dog ferocity.

The last hour was a blur. No more division of passengers and crew, everyone was a bear in a trap, lashing out. All that screaming, that crying at once. If he had to picture hell, it was that ship ripping itself apart and taking everyone down with it.

13 hours

THE WATER WAS RISING, THE beach shrinking, while the sun blazed with blistering heat. He was being fried. His dreads gave him some cover, but he made the woman put a jumper over her head to shade it, otherwise she would broil in this salt-coated frying pan. She thanked him in her language.

His head pounded. Dehydration and tiredness and stress. And he was so hungry. He shouldn't have thought about frying pans. His stomach rumbled so loud she looked up at him.

A raft of plastic bottles bobbed on the surface far out at sea. If they came any nearer he'd swim out there to check. For now he sat next to her on their small patch of sand, and they sucked the sweets while they still had the saliva to do so, and that was enough.

14 hours

NO MORE BODIES FOR A while now. Some indeterminate shapes further out, bobbing with the swell, but too far to swim to.

He'd found a handbag. Soaked, full of water. Dissolving tissues inside it. A small pair of knickers. A purse. A compact mirror. He kept that. It could be useful for signalling. There was also an unopened bar of chocolate. Sealed in plastic so no water could get in. He dumped the bag but ran over to his fellow survivor. He'd found out she was called Tomoko, via the universally understood system of pointing at your chest and repeating a word. He broke the chocolate in half. Well, split it, more accurately, since it was a melted mess. But it was gorgeous. The best he'd ever tasted. He licked his fingers, licked the wrapper, and the smell of the melty cocoa lingered in his nostrils.

Another find: he'd risked the deep water and swum back with the agglomeration of plastic bottles, always glancing warily around as he splashed. One bottle was full, and he was hopeful until he opened it and discovered it to be sea water, entered through a crack. Some were too disgusting to risk, but one was a mineral water bottle, and was half full, and within date, and when he tested it the water wasn't salty. He took a gulp of it, and almost cried that it was gone so quickly. He forced her to drink the other half. Told her she'd die otherwise.

That bottle was likely from the ship, or a passenger. Yet others were weathered, breaking down, label-less. From somewhere else. They'd floated, pulled together into a mass. Why so many of them? Surely that must mean they were near land? You wouldn't just have loads of plastic bottles floating all over the sea.

Something rolling in the water further out. Then it disappeared. Another body? He expected it to reappear but it didn't. He remembered another shape he'd seen earlier, like a corner of dark fabric. He told himself it was a floating umbrella, not a black fin. But he shuddered as the sea rushed in, ushering them back to the rock, the beach now under water.

He wasn't ready for this. Not again. Not so soon.

15 hours

THEY STOOD ON THE HIGHEST point, water lapping over the sharp edges of the ridge, beach vaguely visible as a ghostly hue under the water. The things they'd decided to keep were packed into the suitcase. He used his belt to tie the extendable handle to a loop on his jeans, so that it couldn't drift away.

This time they would stay standing, daylight enabling them to see where they put their feet, to keep their balance and watch out for each other.

She coughed. Somehow that made him want to cough too. Salt was everywhere, a grimy feeling on arms and legs and face. Every time he licked his dry lips with a parched tongue he was reminded of it and it made him gag. They watched the water rise inexorably, now washing up to their feet. He told her it would be fine.

16 hours

THIS MUST BE THE HIGH tide again. They gripped the floating suitcase. The water came up to her breast, his waist. Not so cold this time, with everything scorched by the afternoon sun. They just had to hold on and grit their teeth.

When he looked down he could see the stone they stood on, but distorted by three feet of water. Something moved in one of the lightless crevices that ran deeper below the surface. Maybe crabs lived within the rock.

He talked to her. Perhaps she understood some of it. She listened patiently, anyway, as he talked about rescue, and how lucky they were, and that they mustn't give up hope. And sometimes she replied, and it didn't matter that he couldn't understand the words, it was still good to hear them. To know he wasn't here alone. It was still communication, and took his mind off the rising waters.

Glints of light darted in the sea nearby. Fish, each as big as his hand. They kept their distance for now. But weren't piranhas that size? Did they live in the sea? What if small fish attracted bigger fish?

His heart raced, and he scanned the surface layers of the sea for a dreaded shape, squinting against the bright sun's reflections. He didn't know which was worse: the night-time sea of black all around, as if they sank into freezing tar, a flat world where the things lived below in the unknown cold; or during the day when you had light to see textures, mysterious shapes in the blue that could be tentacled monsters or shifting shadows, poisonous sea snakes or harmless seaweed, while you were surrounded with shades darkening down, implied depths that made you dizzy with vertigo. And the deep drop behind them, vertical black rock, a cold sub-sea cliff face they stood on the edge of, where vision quickly ended. Things came up out of deep water when they got hungry. Everyone knew that.

And then he would look at Tomoko instead, and it would help, and he'd calm as she talked to him in unknown words. Her dark eyes were full of hurt but at least hurt meant life.

17 hours

THE WATER RECEDED AGAIN. IT was down to their knees when he saw what was definitely a plane or helicopter in the sky. Still too far to hear its engines. They waved their arms anyway. The crew might be looking this way with binoculars. But would they see two small bodies and a blue suitcase in all that sea? Then he remembered the mirror and took it out, spilling items into the sea in his haste, and he angled the shiny surface but couldn't tell if he was doing it right, and then the aircraft was only a dot and it was pointless.

He wanted to scream. Had to bite down on his dry tongue. A scream would shred his raw throat.

"They'll be back. The tide will be out next time. Then they will see the island and investigate. We could write our names in the sand." His voice didn't sound like his voice.

20 hours

THE SUNSET WAS BEAUTIFUL. ALMOST made you forget the pain. Blues fading into flamingo pinks. Reminded him of home. So long since he'd been there.

He gathered anything that might be useful into a pile in the centre of the sand. This time they could prepare. Then they sat next to each other and watched the sun sinking. Everything went below the water eventually.

22 hours

IT WAS DARK NOW. THE tide at its lowest level again, giving the freedom of the pale beach which occasionally glittered in the starlight and moonlight. So peaceful, only the gentlest hush of the waves that stroked and sucked against the shore. They had a few hours until the sea levels would rise again.

Tomoko shivered so he draped a spare jacket over her shoulders. The jacket was white, from a dead member of catering staff, and reflected the faint light from the sky. Again, she looked like a ghost.

24 hours

MAYBE THEY'D BEEN WASHED AND blown further away from the sinking ship than he'd expected? You had to bear that in mind. A possibility.

Of course the search teams would work that out, look further afield. They normally did that for days, called in more help. He was sure of it.

26 hours

NIGHT-TIME STILL. SEA COMING IN now. It would be their third time under the water. He didn't know if he could keep doing this. Two high tides a day, that wasn't playing fair. They crammed everything into the suitcase.

"It's dark but we need to stand up again. Stay out of the water as much as possible," he told her. She didn't nod, just followed him up the jagged rocks.

Day 2 some time

IT FELT LIKE DAWN WOULD never come. They both shivered, knocked about by the cold water that half submerged them, and she was coughing again. He took her delicate hand and held it and told her sea otters did that when they slept, to stop them drifting away from each other.

His head pounded nonstop. Hers must be too, but she didn't complain. And the cold water must have sucked more heat from her than from him, she was immersed deeper. That underlined her strength. Focus on that, anything solid to help get through this icy darkness.

Day 2 some time

WHEN IT WAS BRIGHT, AND dry enough to sit on the beach again, he played with the mirror, reflecting little beams of sunlight towards the horizon with shaking hands. Someone might see the light.

Nothing else was being washed up. Everything from the ship dispersed or found or swallowed. No more bodies to move or wreckage to check for anything useful before it got sucked back by the sea.

Tomoko shivered and leaned against him. Once upon a time it would have meant something different. Now, it just made him want to cry. He hugged her. It will be fine. We're alive.

He held the mirror so she could see her reflection. She tried to comb out matted hair with her fingers but gave up. His big fingers would be no good for such a fine task either. Hey, all this sea and sun and salt, you'll get dreads like me. But she didn't smile.

Then he caught his own face in the small circle of glass. It looked drawn, tired, not his own. Such a change in this short time. Or was it a short time? It felt so long already.

Day 2 some time

THE WATER ROSE. TOMOKO WAS coughing bad, real bad, something wrong. Maybe she'd been ill before the accident.

He paced around, couldn't keep his legs still. A few bottles came. Lidless, empty. Water. She needed to drink *water*. Pure, no salt, beautiful, tasteless water. And pills. Antibiotics, painkillers. He wanted to punch the ground, to cry, to shout, but had no energy for that, so he just chewed on the inside of his cheek. He was even angrier because she was so ill but didn't seem to care any more.

Day 2

SHE SHIVERED NOW EVEN IN the sun, even in the dry. The water was killing her. And it was coming back, damn predator, sucking life.

An idea. He took some scraps of plastic bags he'd kept. Ripped them into small sheets. He ground his teeth in concentration. Wetsuits. Water gets in but gets trapped in a layer. Warmed by skin, keeps you warmer.

Only bits of plastic. Less than a binbag.

Put it against your skin, he said. Under your clothes.

He demonstrated, on himself. She wouldn't get up. He tried to shout but it was a scratchy growl. So he said please please and held a bag out, and cried dry, the words made no sounds but she listened and took the plastic, and he turned away in case she had to take clothes off. When she tapped his shoulder the plastic was gone and he lifted her blouse, just to the midriff, yes, it looked right. And he used some strips of material, tied them round her waist and arm, try and hold plastic in place, keep you warmer, he said, have to keep you warm, and the water was pushing them towards the rocks. Day, it was day. Hot but keep her warmer in the water. please, we will get through this, he said it but it was silent.

Day 2?

No one came.

Day 3?

May have lost track of time. No easy way to tell.

Their baked lips were cracked and bleeding. Her pale skin wasn't so good in the sun, burnt red, bad, he made her cover up more.

he would kill for water. literally kill (as long as it was a bad person, not a friend or family or dog)

no need to go toilet any more that's something hahahah no embarrassment at the end of the island

she'd got through the high tide daytime but wouldn't stand now, only lay on the sand and he was exhausted but shuffled in circles as it cooled, and every lap he counted to keep track of time and then checked her to see if she was still alive and he wouldn't move on until he knew she was. he kept losing track of the counting but did it anyway, with his eyes closed. he fell over once.

the water kept coming in and out and in the sun it was too bright to look up for help, and too bright to look down at the sand it reflected all white bright, and in the night it was too dark to see the sky, and the water was too dark to see down

Night

SHE STILL HAD PLASTIC AND he put more on when the water was
cumming in he could shiver and chatter his teeth but she was real
ill he shulda bin a doctor or a nurse not musician

water coming in already again

she wouldn't stand up, he pulled her higher from the water's
edge.

she wouldn't get up

please please

she was breathing

he fell next to her and tried to talk, it was a hoarse whisper but
it was words, sometimes, he could still do words

and he told her his story and he regretted lots he shuld a been
better, no one really loved him because he hadn't bin good, well
his momma thought he was but she would, he was selfish and hed
been bad to women, not bad bad but he lay with them, lots of
them, not just the rich white ones, then he moved on, and he was
fucking a woman on the boat who was also from the caribbean
and she was nice but he was already making a play on another and
they were probably both ded now and he felt awful, maybe it
shulda been him. you get this life and what was he doing? what
was he doing to earn it? and he looked at her and he couldn't talk
to her but he could. and he wouldn't let her go. not this once ever.
because he knew she was good. and he knew she was hurtin and
not just the sick, but that was part of it, maybe it was all
connected and nuthing was chance random, but he guessed she
had a boy and what if he'd been in another boat, think of that

77

huh, how good that would be if she lived and got back with her son, her sun, it would make my life worth sumthin too, cos it was what was important when you got down to it was being good. ive left it too late. but your kid, even if it is dead, i bet it loved you, and you loved it, so you were luckier than me after all, you didn't live all alone like you were the only one that counted, it was a bad way to live, and id lied a lot to everyone and am sorry for that, and maybe if you understood me now id lie but you don't and it makes me true to you. im doing better than you and i don't deserve it, and i blew all my chances to earn it.

and some of the words hadn't come out but he sed them anyway, in his hed, and maybe she heard them because it was just the two of them, where else would the words go

he stroked her tangled hair and did manage to cry a bit, but not for him

he reckoned its only confession if theres someone listening

the water was comin in

she looked at him weakly and he knew shed heard him, some of it, and he eventually managed to get her up the rocks somehow, both so tired, do it again, sit and watch the water, night-time water getting nearer, soon they'd have to stand, he kept his arms round her

A night

WATER UP TO HIS WAIST, all cold, and even the gentle swell now could dislodge him if he wasn't careful, bowl him over the edge into the abyss. He clung to the suitcase, the teeny unexpected liferaft

He clung to her with his other arm but she was slipping

he thought her eyes were close closed

wake up. wake up

he could hardly stand and had to hold her up, she was pulling him down

He unfastened a tie that he'd put round her waist, fed it through the suitcase handle and tightened it, attached it to her, the plastic on her body slidy and wet

she wasn't shivering wasn't coughing

that should be good but it wasn't

more clothes, should have put more clothes on her even though it weighed you down, sucked up the sea, it seemed warmer too, kept it in, have to keep it in

she slipped down, knees gone, under the water, no! he hooked his hands under her armpits and lifted her, she weighed nothing, it was all the water, but

so tired to his arms, sore like head

aches everywhere, she seems so heavy, water so heavy, but have to keep her out of it

he couldn't go on, this pain, it ground him down, if he held her he would die, his knees were ready to buckle,

he lifted her higher, it was no good

so tired

he could let her go

it was what she sought

she just wanted to die.

maybe she was dead

please dont

so cold and stiff, he was holding up a corpse, killing himself for a corpse, but he couldn't check, too dark, taking all he had just to stand there with her

if he let go she'd sink under, drift down the deep sea side of the island and fall forever

join her everliving son

no point holding up her body now, she was killing him too

but he couldn't do it

he couldn't do it

couldnt

didn't want to be alone

and something rough and heavy brushed his leg as it passed and he knew it wasnt her hand it was something else and he kept her tight in his arms

he wouldn't give up for her, wouldn't let the sea have her, she was all he had

up up, he lifted her higher, nearly lost his footing, slipped but stopped before he fell off the ledge, his teeth were chattering

despite fire in his legs and chest, held on in the cold, kept her head above the water and tried to sing a song, one of the ones from the band, something dance hall rithim, distract him, help her soul go somewhere better

but he had forgot every tune

Water going out time

SHE GOT HEAVIER WHEN WATER went down, he had to kneel
and put her stiff body against his shoulder
    Maybe light on horizon, hope
    Could see bit, see water go back, water doin what water did
    and when there was sand and some more light he got moving,
untied suitcase and left it, crawled on his hands and knees slicing
them on the razor edges then gently pulled her body after him,
hands under her armpits again, dragging her feet behind, trying
not to let them drop too hard as they descended
    all so wet and cold and empty, nothing in, like night sky
    but yes, light coming up now
    get her somewhere soft, last place can't be hard wet slimy rock,
he wouldn't allow it
    and when he got to the beach he put her down and climbed
on top of her dead body, give her heat, just in case
    wrapped her in his arms
    you missin this, the sunlight, so beutiful he said, hardly able to
lift his head
    you better than me
    she was so stiff dead, no no, he should move but he can't
    and she groans
    he put an ear to her chest
    A noise and it *was* her, not dead, not dead yet
    and he wanted to cry but laughed instead, rough scary croak
but happy

he got off her, took his jacket off and wrapped her in it, then leaned back against an outcrop, leaned her back against him, the stone diggin sharp in his spine and head but he didn't care no more, at least she could lean back on something soft, he put his arms round her

and when the sun was coming up he shined the mirror, reflected the sun from, so weak but do it anyway because this was the last time he could control it, move that sun in defiance, the last rise they'd see

so beautiful, he said, mouth sandpaper

shine and sleep and do it again on sand

got here together stay together

not worth going on alone

sleep

sleep

woke and felt her chest for heart, she inhaled, raggedy and broken but she was breathing, all okay, sun warming on them both now, all okay to sleep

eyes hardly open but squinted, yeah, sea going out, some time before the last time

sleep

noise buzzing in ears in dream, giant mosquitos wanting to drink their blood, their only thing left, only so loud, get bigger

he looked up from the white beach, a mirage all blurry, eyes swimming and stinging, always stinging on top o everythin else

can't be real, no way, always bein tricked, just needed peaceful time, they sleep shouting can't be real, ruin peace and quiet had for so long, what they would have again forever

and only thing make him look again it the blowing air, swirling, that not feel like dream as his dreads move in breeze unless storm here again, but sun still, not big clouds

in his dream they come they come

if only dreams could come true

and his lips were moving when they tried to separate him from Tomoko, but he wouldn't let her go, his arms gripping on so tight that the crew winched them both up on the stretcher together while the rescuers whooped ecstatic, these two souls finally found on the bone-white beach that had been somehow missed.

It Will Be Quick

HE HELD HIS HANDS OVER her eyes until the last minute.

"There," he said, releasing her.

Pale green like a sun-faded hospital wall.

"I didn't want green," she said quietly.

"Nonsense. It's a good neutral colour, whether it's a him or a her." Michael grinned with satisfaction and patted her tummy. He'd not wanted them to know the sex; so they didn't.

MORNING SICKNESS HIT WITH A vengeance. Always at the most inappropriate moment, such as on a bus or at work. With the general tiredness it added up to feeling rotten most of the time, as if she was ill.

"Don't worry, it will be over quickly, morning sickness passes within a week."

But it didn't. The nausea went on and on, a churning impact on healthy eating – or any eating.

"HAVE YOU SORTED OUT THE leave from work?" Michael's mother asked, bustling around the kitchen as if it were her own.

"Yes," she said. "It will be strange leaving just when I started to enjoy the job."

"It's the way it is, love. You have to get your priorities right, do what's expected."

"I suppose."

"You don't sound convinced but trust me, this is the voice of experience. Your Michael; Myles; Janice. Three times I've been through it. Three glorious times. First is the worst, third's the charm."

"We're only doing this once. We've talked about it."

At the edge of her vision Michael's mother shook her head and grinned.

THE PUB. JUKEBOX MUSIC, THE bleeps of fruit machines, the voices of people: these things swallowed silence.

"Oh you're so lucky! I wish our Daz would give me one!"

"You not gettin' any then, Charlotte?" ribbed Suzie.

"Give me a *baby* I mean, you dirty-minded cow! He's probably shooting blanks, knowing my luck!"

The others burst into raucous drunken shrieks, but she just sat there quietly, listening to their banter, feeling alone even though it was supposed to be a night out celebrating *her* news. She intended to have one drink – one lousy little glass of wine – but Charlotte had overridden her and made her have a fruit juice. "You've got to think about the baby," Charlotte had said. "It's your role now, you lucky cow! Don't worry, you won't have to deny yourself for long – only another six months!"

So she sat like a forgotten toy in a child's room, discarded and apart.

SHE WOKE SWEATING, BUT COULDN'T remember the dream. Again. Just that it was horrible, something to do with suffocation.

She listened for Michael's breathing and was rewarded with a nasal snore.

She didn't know why she felt relief that she hadn't woken him.

IT SEEMED TO BE EVERYWHERE, continually tapping away at her consciousness: the miracle of birth and motherhood. Films, TV programmes, even the adverts; overtly in images and articles in magazines, reinforced with subtext. Conversations overheard, people seen, dramas on the radio, products at the chemist ... How come she had never noticed it before? It was more than tapping, she realised – it was hammer blows of assault.

"Naomi's Baby!" the celebrity magazine screamed at her as she passed the news-stand; image of a tanned, smiling woman holding the puff-faced thing up to the camera.

Later, alone in a public toilet, she touched her belly: but she could not sense the miracle of conception, no matter how much she roamed both hands over the small, rounded surface. She just felt empty.

AT FIRST IT WAS LIKE putting weight on, gradual and inevitable, but she didn't *feel* like she had a baby inside her. Only when it started kicking did the reality sink in.

Early on the kicks made her feel like she was going to break wind, as if her body was out of control and determined to embarrass her.

As the pregnancy progressed something worse developed – somehow it moved around, able to kick her in different places. Harder than before. Under her ribs was the worst, jabbing pains she couldn't ignore.

"I love you," she would say, biting back tears of pain caused by the kick. She held her hands on her tummy, hoping to calm it, but it kicked again and this time she did start crying.

HE LAUGHED WHEN SHE TOLD him later.

"It's natural. Must be a boy if he's a good kicker. My little boy!"

He said the last to her stomach, not to her face. She had noticed that he spoke to that more often now.

THE MIDWIFE GAVE HER A clean bill of health.

"Everything's normal with you and the wee one." The midwife refrained from revealing the sex. Michael's reason for wanting it to be a surprise was so they could both experience "the wonder and miracle of nature".

"And the way I feel?"

"Och, it'll pass before long. Your body's just run down because it's feeding two."

That was it. She was being drained. Wasn't that what parasites did?

The midwife looked into her eyes, considering her.

"Dinna worry, lass," she said. "You'll be a good mother."

Her eyes welled up but she just replied, "Thanks."

BACKACHE. ALL THE TIME. IN her lower back, as if she had carried heavy shopping bags around town. It hit her worst in bed at night, beside his limp body, as if it had stored itself up all day only to release the pain when she needed sleep. But she wouldn't cry.

She had also put on four stone. She wasn't any fatter – it was all in this big lump in front of her, a lump that was always in her vision whatever she looked at, always there in the periphery to remind her of its presence.

TOWARDS THE END SHE TRIED to avoid sitting on anything low such as a sofa, since she couldn't easily get up again. She had a choice of two indignities.

One was to be helped up, with inevitable jokes from someone who found it amusing (making her want to punch them in the face – though she just gritted her teeth and smiled and thanked them after breaking the physical contact as quickly as she could). Sometimes it was Michael who made the jokes; his were about launching ships, and he did it when they had company. She felt betrayed.

The other option was to slide sideways off the sofa onto her knees and to get up that way.

She used to have a gym pass, and a reactive body built from the sweat she paid there. Now she was graceless, her awkward body shape a form of disability.

As a bonus, they told her that there'd be a period when she'd wet herself if she laughed or sneezed because of the pressure on her bladder.

Luckily she rarely laughed any more.

She was thankful for small mercies.

HER OWN MOTHER CAME TO visit, a rare occurrence. They were alone in the kitchen. Her mother smoked by the open back door, cigarette a proudly uncouth statement on her un-PC nature.

"She told you birth is over quickly?" She snorted in disgust on hearing what Michael's mother had said. "Listen, love: what that stuck-up woman said, it's bullshit."

Her mother took another drag and continued her speech while staring out at the grey sky beyond the empty bird feeder.

"The truth is – expect to want to die." She punctuated the last words by stabbing at the air with the cigarette. "That's how it will be. If you expect that level of agony then anything less is a bonus."

They had never been close, but that was the first time in months that she felt anyone had been honest or shared anything with her.

Her mother waited courteously until she had finished crying before stubbing out the butt on the patio and coming back inside.

"WHAT THE HELL ARE YOU doing!" Michael snapped with shock when he caught her. The first time he'd exhibited anything other than smugness or patronising concern since the year had begun.

"Changing the colour of the room. I hated the green." She brandished the red-dripping paintbrush at him but he snatched it out of her hand before she could react.

"Red? It's horrible. Like being in a huge vagina. And in your state you shouldn't be doing *anything*. Come on out. I'll repaint those two walls tomorrow, there's enough green left."

"Why? Why won't you let me do anything? At what point did I stop being a person, Michael?" She didn't want him to see her cry, he always took it for a sign of weakness, but she seemed to have no control any more, even over her emotions. She was just a fat puppet controlled from without and within.

"You're still a person, don't be silly, but you know you mustn't exert yourself, Princess. Come on, let's get you to bed and forget about all this nonsense."

To her shame she was too tired to resist.

THEY'D GONE TO THE HOSPITAL and been put in a labour room with an en suite toilet and shower, designed so everything could be wipe-clean, even bodies.

"I've been feeling ... well, niggly. Just not quite right," she explained as the midwife checked her vital signs. The squeeze of the blood pressure monitor relaxed with a rubbery hiss.

"And I'm her birthing partner," Michael said, proudly.

"Well, I think your contractions have started. That's what you're feeling," explained the midwife.

"But it's not intense?"

"Doesn't matter. They're irregular and light, but still contractions. Is it okay to give you an internal examination to check your dilation?"

She prepared herself for the invasion, gentle and lubricated as it was. The internal movement felt like prodding.

This place terrified her. Unnatural chemical smells. Complete strangers coming and going. Echoes of people crying. Hospitals attempted to convey hi-tech miracles when she knew it was really just about cutting and puncturing with sharp knives then sewing flesh back together.

Michael held her hand but when she looked at him his gaze wasn't on her face, but was on the young and pretty midwife performing the thorough examination.

She broke her hand free.

"Well," said the midwife, smiling as she disposed of the rubber glove. "You're about four centimetres dilated. I also suspect your waters have broken because I can't feel any membrane."

"No, that can't be!"

"It happens. It's not always some mighty gush. Have you had any unexpected leaks?"

"Well, yesterday morning, maybe ... I just thought I'd wet myself."

"That might be it. Over before you know it, or it's a trickle that passes us by. Don't worry, it's normal."

Normal? If the waters had already broken, wasn't that what they called a dry birth? She'd heard tales. Wasn't that more difficult and painful? Wasn't that –

"I'm not ready!" she told the midwife, trying to sit up.

"Doesn't matter. It's the baby decides when you're ready."

SINCE HER WATERS MAY HAVE broken more than twenty-four hours ago, they suggested "active management". She was put on an inducement drip to make the labour quicker and regulate the contractions, and antibiotics to reduce the risk of infection. It connected a vein in her wrist to a tube and a suspended bag, reducing her movement options. Two pads on her stomach monitored the baby's heartbeat and her contractions, connected to a machine by the bed. Both tethers made her a double prisoner of the bed and the baby.

"We'll monitor you and your baby's wellbeing, and your labour can progress naturally as long as it's safe for both of you."

"We'd like that," said Michael, smiling at the midwife. "We want everything to be natural."

The midwife ignored his interruption. "This will make the contractions stronger, so we'll discuss your options for pain relief. Gas and air, painkillers, epidurals."

But Michael never liked being left out of discussions. "Won't that be bad for the baby?" he asked. "Much better if it's more natural, you know, breathing and meditation and stuff?"

This time the midwife did face him.

"It's all fine for the baby, or we wouldn't offer it. And this is a choice for the *mother*. She's the one going through this, not you. Your job is to support her, whatever she chooses. I guess a man's ideal role in pregnancy is no different from in marriage, eh?"

His mouth hung open, and it wasn't an attractive sight, and at that point she could have happily hugged the pretty midwife.

HOURS LATER.

It was impossible to talk during contractions, and her words were interspersed with grunts outside of them. Even language was being imprisoned.

She was six centimetres dilated. During some contractions she would put her hand on her belly and feel the muscles involuntarily harden, the painful urge to expel.

"No, I'm here, been here for the whole thing!" Michael wasn't talking to her, he was speaking into his phone as he strode around the room, having just returned from a coffee break. "Yeah, she's doing fine. Her face is all flushed and sweaty but otherwise she looks okay. No, I'm just that kind of dad. I think all fathers should be involved. It's an equal thing, isn't it? Only fair that we do our share!"

She groaned aloud as the next contraction started. Michael told her he needed to dash out for some more fresh air, but that she was doing great.

ANOTHER FEW HOURS. THE MIDWIFE said her contractions weren't as regular as hoped, but it was all fine. She'd get the obstetrician in to give her a check.

"Maybe it – the baby – doesn't want to come out after all?" she suggested.

"That's just your own fears. The baby wants to meet you. Not long to wait now," the midwife reassured her.

The doctor came in, felt her tummy and examined her internally, then the results made him frown, his bushy eyebrows looking like grey cumuli.

"Well, this explains one phenomenon," he said. "The baby's head is in the pelvis – we already knew that – but the position is what we call OP, occipito posterior. Basically, the baby's back is against your back. This back-to-back position is associated with marginally more complicated births."

"*More* complicated? You're kidding me?"

"Nothing major, just it can take a bit longer, be a jot more painful, a little more tiring. Basically, the baby presents a slightly bigger diameter, so we have to modify things a tad. Don't look so worried, we're used to dealing with this! It's all minor procedures, none of them take long."

The words drifted over her as she tried not to let this complication sink in, tried not to focus on what clinical terms like "presentation" meant to soft tissue.

"We'll move you to the operating theatre – don't worry, it's just a safe place where we can look after you better, a more controlled environment – and get you comfortable. We'll aim to deliver the baby by forceps."

"I don't want to go through with this!" Her eyes darted from the doctor to the midwife to Michael. "Can't you just knock me out, cut it out of me, wake me up when it's – rgggggggg." Another contraction. They all waited, politely, while she became something that lived in a cave, not a suburban house.

Once she was fully human again, the doctor said, "We can do that, though it's not always the better choice. When the baby is head first, like this, most women prefer to try for a natural vaginal birth, with emergency caesarean as an option if that doesn't work. But the final decision is, of course, yours."

Michael was nodding, and told her it was up to her, but she saw it in his face – a face that was so transparent to her today. Disappointment. Judgement. Of course, it wasn't just his, it was everyone's. They all looked down on her ungainly form as muscles took on a life of their own, her toes clenching and reminding her she hadn't varnished her toenails because THIS

WAS NOT MEANT TO FUCKING HAPPEN YET so even that was taken from her, and this was something that would happen once, only once ever, they talked about it, never again, never never afuckinggain, and so whatever she did today would be the choice she always carried, that they always judged her on, that would also determine what she felt about herself.

She still didn't feel like a mother. She wanted to, but didn't. Maybe this would help. Perhaps if she went through it, she would experience something other than kicks and prods. Because if she didn't spark something soon, now, possibly it would never ignite, never form properly, just be an *association* not a *connection*, and that would be the worst thing to be judged on. Not to be a woman. Not to be a mother.

"Go ahead," she said. "We'll try it the natural way."

"You're so brave," said Michael. "And I remember reading that being tranquil will help create a quicker birth. Maybe you need to relax more, and that would help?"

"I *am* fucking relaxed!" she yelled, as another contraction hit.

THEY MOVED HER INTO THE brightly lit theatre, and she discovered "getting you comfortable" included a spinal anaesthetic. She lay on her side, knees pulled up, wincing as as the sharp spike jabbed about inside her back, but terrified of moving. That was the "mild discomfort" they warned her about. Just another invasion into private places as the needle injected chemicals into her cerebrospinal fluid, bodily liquid in intimate contact with her brain, the only world where she could be her true self. Could she trust her mind after that, or would it be anaesthetised too?

But ten minutes later she was thankful as her lower body numbed. The contractions still came, though they felt more distant than before, as if someone else was doing them for her. That was a relief. She was knackered, sweaty and thirsty, and she only wished it was Michael that took half the pain, that felt it, except he wasn't there, hadn't been holding her hand or in a supporting position since her screaming had started. She would love to have him there during the next contraction so she could scream at him to *fuck off* and slap his face with her words, that face so easily offended by the *vulgar*, as he'd put it, that face unsuited to the deep smell of her body and what it leaked at the moment, that face she would like to smack with her hands again and again as she gritted her teeth during this almighty tensing that seemed to go on for minutes each time, even though it was shorter than that, they told her so it must be true, only forty-five seconds, what did they know, what did they fucking know? She wanted him there to send him away. Foiled. She had to make do with her audience of medical people, all watching, encouraging her, as if she were a racehorse with her legs up on blue stirrups, or an entertaining quiz show where contestants wore no underwear.

"That's it, your cervix is fully dilated," said the doctor, after his latest exploration.

"It's about time when you'll feel like pushing," said the midwife, holding her hand in Michael's place.

"It may be a little harder, because of the spinal," said the doctor.

"But it will start, once the baby's in position," said the midwife.

"So we're going to make a small cut," the doctor continued, like they were in some kind of double act.

The words sank in, and broke the passive reception of their voices.

"A cut?" she asked, not liking the word. Cutting. Things separated. Things removed. Ending up as less than she was before.

"It's called an episiotomy, a small cut through the vaginal wall and perineum to make the vaginal opening bigger."

"Why? Babies fit, don't they?"

"If you remember, the baby is facing up, occipito posterior, which is fine, but to make it safe we'll be using forceps, so there has to be room for those *and* the baby's head."

She started crying. The midwife squeezed her hand.

"You'll be fine," continued the doctor. "It's all safe, we'll numb the area before, then stitch you up afterwards. It will speed things up."

They seemed surprised when those words made her cry even more.

THE NEXT COUPLE OF HOURS were the worst.

She knew she sometimes fought it, clenching rather than pushing, because she kept picturing cuts, and tears, and imagining dryness, and the epidural took away some control so whatever she did, her efforts felt as weak as her goosebumps-covered thighs.

She'd never known she could sweat so much, this put gym workouts to shame, same as her bursts of swearing would have put Michael to shame if the bastard toerag was there.

And when they took out the huge, curved tongs, she wondered how they would fit those unnatural things in, smooth stainless steel or not. She screamed, and pushed, and they pulled, and there were problems, their faces showed it, and amidst the agony she heard one mention something that sounded like "failed forceps", and she wished they had knocked her out, unconscious, removed it while she was somewhere else, wish she'd not tried to be brave, it was pointless, she saw that now, pushing pushing, even with no strength left to push, and what if it was partway out but got stuck, what cuts would they do then, what cuts were left to do, would they reach inside her tummy and try to scoop the head back in, not just fingers inside her, not just metal curves, but whole stranger's hands, it certainly felt like that, don't look, the contracting closing-in pain again, and the outward-going splitting pain like her insides were being torn out, except pain was too small a word for THIS fucking torture.

And then she did it, something she hadn't done for over twenty years – she called out for her mum, and her mum was not there, her blood an undependable absence, and when you got down to it she was as alone as she'd ever been, even in this room, because hurt is always faced alone, learn that as a kid and learn it well, because you can grit your teeth and better understand the knocks you'll get, then it won't be such a shock, won't be like this emptiness.

And then it was over, just like that.

They handed her the baby.

She held it. A girl, after all. Such a tiny blood-soaked thing in the wake of all that suffering.

She counted its fingers and toes, handed it to the midwife when she was satisfied.

All that effort, and it was over, just like that?

EXCEPT, IT WASN'T.

She could hardly focus on the pronouncements as they worked, still in the bright lights torture room, she was floating, high, didn't notice which phrases were directed at her, which at other medical staff, which were important, which not, which were in human language, which alien. They all washed over her the same, as she drifted beneath the waves of painkillers. She didn't even know if it was day or night.

Blood loss. Third-degree vaginal tear. Postpartum haemorrhage. Perineum. We'll sort you out in a jiffy. Obstetric anal sphincter injury. Low iron levels. Two litre transfusion. It's good news you were already in the operating theatre. Back passage. No long-lasting complications. Repair. Time to heal. Temporary catheter to drain the bladder. Stitches can irritate. Urinary and anal incontinence. Soreness when walking or sitting, so many nerves involved. Avoid sex until the stitches are healed and bleeding stopped.

That got through her brain, somehow. Her mouth was too cotton-woolly, otherwise she'd tell them *that one* was a laugh. She was never having sex again.

LATER.

Michael was gone. She was in her own room because of the extensive stitching and blood loss. A drip still snaked into her arm and the baby was in a small cot by her bed.

She was groggy, and achy, but couldn't sleep.

The hospital was hushed. Soft light crept into the room through the interior window which enabled midwives on the ward to glance in.

Occasionally the quiet tread of a midwife passed; sometimes they came in to see if everything was okay. More often they didn't. Perhaps they assumed she was asleep as she lay in the shadows of the pale ward light.

She struggled to raise her body and reach over to take the baby in her arms.

It was wrinkly. What looked like small patches of white grease on its scalp. A smell of hospitals.

No love swamped her breast. It just felt like she held an old man in miniature, long years compressed within it; her own long years stretching out ahead, years where life and thought orbited this new creature instead of herself, years of denial in order to fulfil the role of "a proper mother" to the satisfaction of everyone.

Only yesterday she had been a girl, it seemed; dreaming of carving a shining life into history, a cut so deep and blindingly bright she would be remembered for it. She had once wanted to make a difference, not be the same as everyone else. What happened?

What *had* happened? Everything. The steel teeth of society, relationships, husband, roles, family, friends, masks, hormones, and every other jagged edge that caught and held her in a vice of attrition.

All had let her down. And as she gazed on the needy life-sucker she held, she knew with a liberating wash of shame that she did not love it.

But that didn't mean she could ignore its feelings. She knew that. It wasn't her own life of dutiful abnegation she should be thinking of.

This girl. This seedling. She would follow her mother; dream her own dreams only to see them slip away, too; career begun then dropped; sacrifice. A pattern repeated and new chains forged. A long-drawn-out affair of cruelty and moulding and oxidising until the shine was gone. No, that was too cruel to wish on anyone.

She pulled a pillow from behind her back. One thing she could do before she slept. Before returning it to the cot.

It would be quick.

Hell's Bean Curd

"HELL'S BELLS, ALFIE, LOOK AT her! What kind of deranged mind would choose orange skin? Her eyebrows look drawn on, and her eyelashes resemble exploding caterpillars. Pass me a knife."

"It's just fake tan, dear."

"No one's fooled by that. Why can't they model their looks on someone nice, like that Katie lady?"

"Katy Perry?" suggested Mr Barrett. While Miriam's attention was focussed elsewhere he took the opportunity to savour the cafe's glorious aroma of frying bacon and eggs.

"Don't be ridiculous, she's American."

"Katie Price?"

"Take your mind from the gutter, Alfred. You're dribbling. I know what you like to stare at."

"I don't stare at –"

"No, the big boaty one ..." The pleasant murmur of conversation, the gentle clinking of cutlery, the fairy-like tingling of the bell above the door, all peaceful sounds – then Miriam thrust a finger forwards. "Ah, Katie Winslet. The English rose. I'll have the sugar."

This wasn't Mr Barrett's ideal day, but there would be more peace later if he agreed to go shabby chic shopping in Shrewsbury now. Doing the deed was as tiring as saying it. At least when they stopped in a cafe he could watch other people. Ideally the sad ones: the arguing couples, the bored teens, the grumpy oldies. It always made him feel better. £1.85 for a cup of catharsis wasn't a bad deal.

The waitress brought their soups. As she took out her pad and moved to the next table Miriam called, "And the bill." Well, more a command than a call. Poor waitress. Literally taking orders all day. He knew the feeling. Alfie dunked his bread without enthusiasm.

"I wanted white bread like you," he said.

"Stop sulking. You know brown is better for you. It's a good job you have me to choose your food. I dread to think what you'd eat if you were here alone."

Chips sprang to mind. Maybe even Miriam's nemesis: French fries.

The couple on the next table dithered over the options. Alfie could see one of Miriam's ears twitching. The man wanted a double-burger bap but they eventually both opted for braised tofu salad.

"Tofu!" Miriam said, leaning forward, but forgetting to lower her voice. "That's neither fish nor fowl." Thankfully the easy-listening music was quite loud. Miriam looked at the menu, checked the price, then drummed her fingers on the tabletop. "Such a fuss over vegetarians. No one makes a fuss over me for not eating mushrooms."

Always best to keep quiet. At least the brown bread seemed to absorb more soup than the white. Alfie was quite proud of its dollop-holding ability. Like a sponge. Would it suck up tea as well? He was tempted.

Food was served at the next table and Tofu Man tucked in. His phone rang. He talked at the same time as chewing, rather an angry call. Miriam held back on tutting for at least ten seconds. Tofu Woman left her partner for the toilet; if she'd had eyes in the back of her head she'd have noted Miriam's slow up-and-down assessment.

"Not so much a hairdo as a hair don't," she pronounced, straightening her back.

No one ever passed the up-and-down test. It was a good job Miriam wasn't the head of an examination board. The nation's kids wouldn't have a GCSE to rub between them.

The last of the bread mopped around his bowl, clearing the final smears of cream of tomato and revealing the plain pottery beneath the neon orange. Could have done with a more generous portion but it was tasty, he had to give them that. If only he could persuade Miriam to go to the toilet too, so he could grab a cream cake from the counter and shove it in his gob before she got back

...

Commotion on the next table. Tofu Man started gasping and dropped his phone, which skittered along the floor. People turned and conversation ceased. He flailed, one hand on his chest – no, throat now, gripping it – trouble breathing as he kicked his legs out. The waitress rushed over while others only stared, forks halfway to gaping maws.

"Are you okay?" the young waitress – just a girl, really – asked the man in a worried tone, getting no response. His face reddened and he collapsed lower in his chair. Now the waitress looked like she would panic. "Someone call a doctor ... no, an ambulance ... I'll do it ... oh shit!" Her hands wavered uncertainly while the man thrashed, then she was rushing to the till when a palm – suddenly thrust out at chest height – stopped her.

Miriam's hand.

"He's choking," said Miriam, as she stood. "Tofu. I saw it all. It's a health hazard. Stuck in his throat. No need for an ambulance. I know the Heimlich Manoeuvre. It will free the food. Never fails if you do compressions properly."

All eyes on her now. She strode over to Tofu Man with authority, arms out as if to keep a crowd back. He had started to go purple, reached for his wife's side of the table, maybe to seize it, to try and stand.

"Are you sure?" asked the waitress.

"Absolutely. I work in a hospital."

"But Miriam," Alfie said, "you're a clean–"

"Hsst! I know my first aid, Alfred."

She seemed solid, an indomitable figure of certainty and awe to the other diners, who now had the luxury of not having to take action. They could just enjoy the show, no doubt readying themselves for applause at the appropriate time. Miriam would love that.

She patted Tofu Man's back. Then she reached around his chest from behind, gripped one fist in the other, and made jerky thrusts up under his ribs.

The man's eyes widened, but nothing flew out of his mouth, pale and rubbery or otherwise. He struggled but was too weak to resist the force of Miriam.

"It will come out soon," she said, yanking harder. Another diner stood, but seemed uncertain how to help. Miriam heaved and heaved but didn't get anywhere. In fact, the man appeared to have passed out.

"Miriam ..." said Alfie.

"Nearly there!" she gasped.

She was going purple herself now, and fell onto her back. Fair play, she kept hold of Tofu Man, and continued squeezing and yanking even as she lay on the floor with him on top of her.

"Stop being stubborn, you silly man!" she yelled as her hands pumped away. For once it wasn't Alfie she was shouting at.

The waitress tried to help but got hissed at. Miriam's skirts had ridden up her thighs far beyond what was acceptable but she squeezed on with the determination of a crocodile wrestler as they skittered across the floor, bumping other tables in Miriam's increasingly ferocious dislodging attempts.

The toilet door opened – Tofu Woman was back. She rushed over to the commotion.

"Harry! Harry!"

"Under control!" Miriam managed to get out in tired bursts, resisting the woman's attempts to remove Miriam's arms from around her husband.

"What are you doing! Didn't anyone give him his aspirin? Harry! Harry, can you hear me?"

"Aspirin?" Alfie asked.

"For his heart – this is the second heart attack in a month."

"Heart attack?" Miriam finally released her death grip.

"Yes! How long will the ambulance be? Why are you all staring at me? You did call one, didn't you?"

The waitress paled, shaking her head and pointing at Miriam, who was crawling towards the cafe entrance on hands and knees.

"He could be dead in a few minutes! GET AN AMBULANCE NOW! EVERY SECOND COUNTS!" screamed the woman.

Among all the sudden tumult, scraped chairs, shouts, jabbed keypads and people crowding round, it was possibly only wide-eyed Alfie who noticed the tinkle of a bell as the cafe door swung shut. It's also possible that no one heard him when he air-pumped a fist and announced, "Hell's bells, she's killed someone! That's grounds for a divorce."

Sweet Nothing

"YOU DIRTY LITTLE BASTARD! LEARN to wipe your fucking arse properly!" She shook him by the arm as she scolded. "Do you think I've got time in the day to always be washing your dirty undies?"

The offending linen was brandished, shaming him as he stood shivering in his vest.

"You can put these on again and make do, I'm not using the washing machine just because you're a dirty little boy. What are you?"

"A dirty little boy."

She threw yesterday's underwear at him; as soon as she left the room he slipped it on and tried not to make a noise while he cried. He didn't want her to shout at him for being a blubber baby too.

AT THE FRONT DOOR SHE clicked open her purse and took out one silver coin.

"I don't even think you deserve this." She put it into his duffle-coat pocket anyway.

He said, "Thanks, Mum," and kissed her cheek when she leaned forward. Another mother walked past, and his mum smiled at the woman and shouted something and pulled his hood up, one of the things she only did when other people were around.

"It's cold. Go," she commanded, the words not giving him any warmth.

HE TURNED THE COIN OVER and over. 10p. He got it every morning. Sometimes in the past he used it in the school tuck shop, but the only things he bought there were chocolate-coated YoYo biscuits, and they were three pence each. The solitary penny left over seemed somehow messy. He *tried* not to be messy.

"Are you coming into the shop?" Freddy asked, nodding at the newsagent's outside the school gates. "Get a penny mixup?"

He followed Freddy in to the mixup counter where tubs and boxes of every tempting colour were spread out below the glass top. Look but don't touch. Every child knows that treasure is always guarded. Sometimes by locked chests, sometimes by dragons, and often by a Mr Morris behind a counter.

"What do you boys want?" asked Mr Morris.

Freddy had 25p, so his white paper would be filled to splitting point as he touched the glass counter, smearing boy-prints in order to make *absolutely sure* there was no ambiguity, no mistakes that could cost a precious penny.

"Two fizzy cola bottles ... and two normal."

The boy could immediately taste the eye-scrunching sourness of the fizzies as they tipped into his friend's bag.

"Three white chocolate drops ... a milk bottle ... a chewy banana ... two blackjacks ... some cherry lips ... a pink fish ... two flying saucers ... a chewy dummy ring – no, can I have that green one? Oh, and a snake ..."

The mouth-watering list went on.

A selection was the most exciting, but other temptations offered themselves. Sherbet dib-dabs always got a crowd at playtime, other kids wanting to stick a wet finger in for a sharp fizz, whether it was the cheaper bag with the red lollipop, or the thick firework-like tube of the liquorice dib-dab. A dinosaur egg gobstopper cost a full 10p but came in its own box and would last more than one playtime of furious, juicy sucking. The ultimate luxury was the current craze – space dust, small in quantity but great in effect as it crackled and popped explosively on the tongue, pinging off the roof of your mouth in shrapnel-spitting bursts.

Any of those would help him get through the morning lessons as he looked forward to eating them at playtime, when they would take away the taste of the smelly milk bottle.

The thought of dinner would help him to keep going after that (as long as it didn't turn out to be yucky fish pie), and then afternoon would be the penultimate challenge, mostly a battle with tiredness and renewing hunger, before the final task of sneaking out of school and getting home without running into big Paul Barrett from the year above, who would spit on him and call him freak or cunt; who would shove a handful of sneezy grass into his face in summer and face-chafing snow in winter, leaving his skin raw and redder than usual.

Sometimes even that was better than going home.

SATURDAY. UNDER HIS BALLED-UP SOCKS, reaching to the very back of the drawer, his heart beating faster, the fear that he would find nothing but more socks – but then his fist closed on the bag and he sighed. The ever-present battle to hold back tears was won.

He piled up the 10p pieces as he counted them. Three piles of ten. He hadn't miscounted. Three pounds. It had taken six weeks to save this up, six weeks of denial. Three hundred fizzy cola bottles ... a hundred and fifty pink shrimps ... or thirty dinosaur eggs' worth of painful restraint.

He pocketed the coins.

"UP THERE." HE POINTED TO the top shelf, where the cellophane-wrapped treasure chests sat. He shook his head as Mr Morris worked his way along the shelf ... no, not the Terry's gold-coloured box, or the Black Magic ... As Mr Morris touched the purple box with the swirly writing, the boy nodded. Milk Tray, not those others which were bitter dark chocolate.

"Lucky boy," said Mr Morris as he wiped dust off the wrapper.

The boy's face scrunched with serious concentration as he counted out the money while Mr Morris folded the box in tissue paper.

"You kids and sweets," said Mr Morris as he took the money and carefully checked it, whilst also shaking his head as if disgusted. "Don't eat them all at once, you'll make yourself sick."

THE BOY HELD HIS STOMACH as he got to his front door, legs unsteady. The empty chocolate box was clenched in his small fist, tissue paper trailing down messily.

He knocked on the hard door and heard muttering and cursing inside as his mum came to let him in.

The taste in his mouth was horrible. He was trying not to cry.

She yanked open the door but her usual glare of dirty-undie disgust softened to puzzlement as she took in his bloody, swollen face and ripped clothes.

He held out the crushed box, picked up from the gutter where it had been thrown by big Paul Barrett after he'd eaten the chocolates while the boy struggled to get them back despite the punches to his face and kicks to his shins, blows he could ignore 'cos they only hurt on the outside.

"Got them for you, Mum. I'm sorry." He couldn't stop the tears this time.

She fell to one knee and gripped his shoulders hard, fingers digging in. He looked into her eyes, expecting the usual gobstopper hardness, but it was gone, sucked away to nothing.

"Marty?"

The expression on her face: he'd never seen it before, didn't recognise it. She drew him in and squeezed so tight he couldn't breathe.

How I Wonder What You Are

WHAT GOES DOWN MUST GO up. That was the rule in this old country that existed before they invented the word "flat". Ed freewheeled down the road, having to brake and waste energy on the curves whilst she disappeared round the bend ahead, riding more efficiently. And he knew what came next.

He glared at the subsequent rise that climbed up into grey skies forever. He dropped into a low gear ready for it but began pedalling too soon and his feet flew off the pedals as they spun and whacked his calf. The bike had been out to get him from the start. Even Scottish hire bikes hated the English.

He eventually got his feet back on the pedals and started gaining on Kayla. That meant she was slowing down. Giving him a chance. So demeaning. She was still in front – it would be too obvious if she let him pass – and his view was basically her purple-clad bum and pink trainers pumping away. He gritted his teeth and kept going, the bike dragging on the ascent, gravity wanting to pull him back, stop him achieving anything. She looked round every so often. Tried to speak to him.

"I'm concentrating," is all he said. All he needed to say. She kept quiet until they reached the top and pulled into a layby for a breather. Again, it was really only for him.

He took his cycle helmet off, letting the breeze cool some of the sweat from his shaved head. He checked his phone for the time, noted the poor signal with a tut, then took a pill from its plastic bubble and washed it down with lukewarm water.

"You get such a great view from here." She stood astride her cross bar, leg muscles taut. "Look at all the whin."

He eyed the bushes bursting in yellow. One of the few plants he recognised.

"Gorse."

"Kissing will go out of fashion when it stops flowering."

Was that a hint? "I'd enjoy the view more if there wasn't any litter." He pointed at a McDonald's milkshake carton with straw stuck out top like a fast-food grenade that someone had dumped by the verge. "It's like they don't give a shit."

"Will you *please* try and see something positive?" she said quietly, without turning to look at him.

"I am trying."

"Try harder."

She started cycling. He fumbled his water bottle back into the carrier, helmet back on, disliking the dampness of the sweat-soaked sponge. He winced as he put his weight on the seat. They were like an ancient torture method, where every rattle of the road translated into vibrating crotch shocks.

The road here was edged with fir trees, all tangled and sprouting fungus – correction, lichen. Mustn't forget last night's lecture.

"I *am* making an effort," he said, after pedalling hard to catch up so that they whizzed alongside each other on the narrow road. "I came here, didn't I?"

"Under duress."

"And I'm out doing your kind of thing."

"After I finally got you to turn off the laptop. Otherwise you'd still be at the cottage, pissing into the Twitter stream."

It had been work, not leisure, but he let it go. A few moments without words, just the whirring of wheels. He actually preferred that.

"It's just ... you never want to do things with me," Kayla said, unwilling to let it drop. "I have to push you. *Every time.* It's exhausting. What's the point of a relationship if I have to do that?"

Oh boy. He had to cycle *and* negotiate these treacherous waters, where one slip sent you into the deep and ball-shrivelling icy murk of a loch. He made a point of speaking slowly, and trying to keep irritation out of his voice.

"You have a relationship because you love someone. It doesn't mean I want to do things with you all the time. We both have our own interests. It can't always be like when you first start going out. You get that rush, you do anything, you're always there, fucking all the time – now *that's* exhausting. It couldn't last.

Would burn out. So it scales back, becomes more realistic. Life isn't romcoms and Hollywood."

Silence. That was good. Certainly good not to have to talk *and* cycle. He was heavier than her, had to work harder. Needed all his puff. Perhaps she was okay after his pep talk. He could lighten the tone, get things flowing again.

"I'll admit I was a bit down on the place. It is pretty. Maybe I could get used to *Skirtland*."

Nothing. Shit, he'd been working on that joke for ages, especially the close-to-native pronunciation.

"Y'know," he added, "because both the men and women here wear skirts."

Still nothing. He wasn't even allowed to make a joke. Robbed, again. Bad enough that she chose this day out. A chance to show off her superior fitness, maybe. Yeah, rub it in. She was always saying he should get off the computer and get outdoors. What was so great about being devoured by midges? It was like when she offered to pay for the whole holiday, because she earned more. Might as well just cut his balls off with a knife. Even her hair trailed out from under her cycle helmet, dark curls that seemed uncontrollable, showing off as they waved wild in the wind, taunting him for the fact that he'd started going bald ...

No. He was being ridiculous. Had to stop thinking like that. Negative leads to negative, a reinforcing spiral, catch it in time to break the downward line. They were going slow enough that he could look around without falling off. Take in some of the land. She'd test him later, ask about his "favourite part", so he needed to stock up.

"Hey, look," he said, pointing to the right. "A fox."

She saw as it faded from view. "No, it's a pheasant."

"You sure? It looked red, with a tail, and ran off."

"Pretty sure. The sheep are too close, they wouldn't be there with lambs around in May if it was a fox."

She was probably right. Grew up in this kind of environment. He had more knowledge of coding and coffeeshops than clans and countryside.

"You know a lot. You miss Scotland?" he asked.

"Aye."

She normally answered with "Yes". Her faintest-of-faint Scottish accents had become a lot more pronounced in the past few days.

"Even though you were only a girl when you all moved to England?"

"Even though."

"You want to move back here?" No answer, but that can be an answer. Shit. Still, his attempt at showing an interest worked. She was smiling.

"Ed, can I borrow your phone?" she asked.

"You've got one."

"I forgot to charge it."

Typical. First thing he did in a hotel room was connect his gadgets to the multi-charger he took with him. She was always "Na na na, let's look around first, na na na do it later, don't be such a spoilsport." Yeah, well, it was the spoilsport who had a fully charged phone, wasn't it?

"What do you want it for? There are no games on it."

"It's for ringing ahead, give them an ETA for when we'll arrive. I said we'd do it en route."

Stay in her good books, and take the chance for a rest. They would pull over to do the exchange. The roads were often single width, but lots of passing places were gouged or blasted out of the steep roadside banks. She skidded her bike to a halt in one, gravel crunching dramatically. Trees leaned over the road from a mossy slope. On the other side it dropped down to marshy land with a stream running through it, broken into sub-streams by raised bush-covered clumps.

But first she scanned around like she'd never seen a tree before. She always did that. They all looked the same to him.

"With sunglasses on that patch of light looks fantastic," she said, pointing at a break in the foliage.

"Oh."

"Try it." She proffered her expensive shades. He hadn't bothered bringing any, since he'd expected it to be raining all the time. He slipped her glasses on.

"Wow!" he said, after a second's pause.

"Told you!"

"Yeah! It looks exactly the same. Only darker!"

She pulled a face and snatched the glasses back, called him a prick, but it wasn't real annoyance.

They ate sandwiches. He finished off with a bar of chocolate, Kayla with an apple. He knew he was winning on that one. Then she took his new iPhone. He made sure she zipped up her cycle jacket pocket after putting the mobile in. Total pain up the arse to get repaired if it was dropped. You couldn't even change the battery in the things any more and –

"What are you thinking about?" she asked.

"Huh?"

"You look so thoughtful. The scenery?"

"Oh, yes, I was just thinking about the scenery. It's good to get out. You know, see all this stuff. The trees and the grass and all that."

He must have sounded convincing, because she was still smiling.

"We making good progress?" he asked.

"Probably done eight miles."

"Is that all? Feels like more."

"Twenty to go."

Oh shit. The distance hadn't sounded like much when she'd looked up from her map, string in hand, and first suggested incorporating cycling into the holiday. He could have driven that in no time.

"I need a pee," she announced. "Tell me if any cars come."

She scrambled up the steep bank, toes digging into moss, hands gripping onto the rocky outcrops. She looked athletic. He'd have lost his footing and slipped down. Screw that. He wouldn't have tried. He'd have just pissed over the fence on the other side of the road, added his stream to the one babbling along below.

"You all right?" he asked.

"Aye." She was mostly out of sight of the road unless you knew where to look. She squatted but used one hand to keep hold of a branch for stability on the steep slope. There was no wind in this sheltered area, but that meant midges. He scratched at his head and neck as the clouds of black menace made tiny incisions in his skin.

"Wow!" she called.

"Laid an egg?"

"No. There's a track up here, and scrapings. Badger, I reckon, looking for earthworms or pignut. They do that spring and summer."

"Great, but there's someone coming. Can't see it yet but heard the engine. Sounds like a school bus."

"Fuck."

"Bet they've all got binoculars and cameras."

She tugged her leggings up, straightened her top, then began a hurried descent.

"Watch where you step," he added. "Rivers run downhill."

A Transit-type van came round the corner from behind. The front seat had three blokes in a line. Ed stared at them while the van passed, and they stared back at him. The sides of the van were just windowless white panels. Off-white in this case, with mud splattered around the wheel arches. Kayla was down to the road now as the van approached the corner that would take it out of sight, but it suddenly braked, pulling up against the steep bank ten feet away. Then it just sat there, engine rumbling. Ed could imagine them watching him in the wing mirrors. They couldn't use the central rearview because the glass on the van's back door was boarded up.

"What is it?" Kayla asked.

"Shush."

Ed kept staring, refusing to cave in first. The sound of a window winding down. Then one of them shouted something without looking back. It was obviously directed at Ed or Kayla. Sounded like an insult, but with the Scottish accent, who knew?

"I beg your pardon?" Ed shouted back, taking a step towards the van. Blue exhaust smoke trailed out in cigar-like puffs.

Kayla put a hand on his arm. "Leave it. Please."

He stopped, but kept his eyes ahead. The red tail-lights glowed and the engine chugged like a watching dragon. Ed gestured that they should move on, flapping his hands dismissively.

After a few seconds a bloke leaned out of the window, black beanie crammed down above too-big ears.

"Are ye lookin at me, or chewin a brick? Either will cost ye bost teeth."

"What?"

"Ye heard. Nice arse ye got there. Not you, ya prick." Laughter from van. "Ah'd give her a pure fuckin if she wants to get in us van. All three o us gan hae a go."

Ed broke free of Kayla's arm and ran towards the vehicle. The bloke retracted his head and the van lurched forward before Ed reached it, leaving a stink of badly burnt fuel. Ed stopped and the vehicle screeched to a halt on the bend, waiting, the same distance between them. They'd drive on if he ran again. Ed knew their tricks. Instead he looked around then picked up a stone off the ground, reached back to throw it.

The van roared off again, around the bend, but Ed spotted the fist thrust out of the side window, middle finger extended upwards. He gripped the stone tight, sharp edges pressing into his hand, then let it drop into the muddy trickle at the edge of the road.

Footsteps.

"What was that all about?" Kayla asked, pulling him round to face her.

"They were cretins."

"Do you know how stupid that was? Trying to provoke people?"

"I wasn't trying to provoke them. Just protecting you."

"From what? Some people pulling into a layby? They might have been checking a map."

"You see it your way, I'll see it mine. Hear what they shouted? They weren't nice people."

"I'm sure you picking up a stone didn't help."

"That was after."

She walked back to the cycles, her shoulders bunched. He followed. She was muttering to herself.

"Nothing happened. It's fine. They've gone," he said. "Can we get back to normal?"

She turned on him. "Normal? How can anything be normal when you misinterpret things? Other people. Me. *Everything*. You always do. Paranoid."

"I'm not paranoid."

She pointed to his pocket. "Have you –"

"Yes. Earlier."

"You were still being aggressive."

"For fuck's sake. Paranoid *and* aggressive? Or just one of them? Which one? Or something else? I bet you've got more you could add." No answer. "Well, what *do* you think my main problem is?"

"If there was only one, it wouldn't be a problem."

He snatched his bike and climbed on.

"Wait. I'm sorry," she said. "That was cruel."

He started pedalling. She didn't follow. Fine. He wouldn't look back. Wouldn't wait. Keep going until he could burn out whatever was shorting inside, sparks of scorching plastic that he had to take far away from anything combustible.

HE CYCLED HARD, WORKING IT out of his system by stomping down on the pedals again and again and again and a-fucking-gain. The borders of the road hemmed him in. It was either wet ditch, steep wooded banks, drystone walls, or routes lined with wire netting and wooden fences, the skeletal grey wood posts weathered smooth by time. A clear message to him: stay on the road, you English bastard.

His breathing came hard and he sweated during long stretches when the sun was on him, replaced by sweet relief whenever passing through refreshing shade. Focus on that, accept it, see the coolness as positive.

Another side road. Blurred image as he flashed past, something white parked there. A van? The van? His bike wobbled and he faced front quickly. Nothing to do anyway. He remembered the advice, took breaths as deep as his burning lungs would allow. And as he cycled he did absorb something of the peace and beauty that comes from isolation.

Why was it so difficult to admit that to Kayla?

Ed's route wound left and right as well as up and down, the road like a giant snake slithering over the land, with so many curves he lost all sense of direction. He slowed now, anger and energy spent, giving Kayla the chance to catch up. Ed glanced back but saw no sign of her purply pinks yet. He eased on the brakes and came to a halt. Got off and leaned the bike against a tree. Took hefty gulps from the water bottle. Tepid.

Still no sign of her following. She must be *really* annoyed.

Another forlorn loch rippled here. He wandered over to a dented sign. Loch Duntelchaig. Okay, that was pronounceable. Just. He stood at the edge of the lapping grey waters. Ringing the view were the browny-grey humps of mountains, washed out and faded by distance. They didn't quite look solid. A wave of unreality. So hard to see things as they were. Stuff gets in the way. She'd told him what the peaks were called while pointing their route out on the map last night, lying in her underwear, but Ed was busy with email. He'd forgotten the names. Were they something like Marilyn Munroe? That was a stupid name for a mountain. Yet he now felt a pang of guilt that he hadn't paid attention. That he didn't put down the laptop and stroke her skin. Kiss her. Appreciate what was there. She always said you had to do that before it was gone.

If he wasn't careful, he'd lose her.

Deep inhale through his nose, slow exhale through mouth. Repeat, times ten. Yep, he was centred now, recovered far faster than used to be the case. That was improvement. Was it this place? Or practice? Didn't matter. It was good news. He needed to share it. Apologise sincerely. Ask her questions about every fucking tree and bush and feathered or furry beastie; then top it off by listening to the answers.

He'd just climbed astride his bike when a drone in the distance stood out as man-made infiltration, not part of the natural soundscape. Eyes pulled towards the thing that was different. A vehicle. White, coming from behind, swallowing the road between them. A grubby van. It decelerated on approach. The road here was straight, so there was no reason to slow. More than one person in the front. Yes, three pairs of eyes on him. He glared back. Instinctive, like hackles rising. The window wound down. Ed tensed. Motion. Something flew out of the side window at him. He tried to dodge but tripped because of the bike between his legs, overbalanced by the single heavy pannier, falling as dirty junk food cartons and empty cans assaulted him with a clatter. Laughter as the van roared off.

He scrambled up and started pedalling after it, full effort, almost catching up but they kept ahead, teasing, and thumping came from inside the van, they were banging on the panels and goading him, and it worked because *fucking hell, if he caught up to the bastards* ... He was close but not close enough, and the road started to climb, and although he went through the gears it was still impossible, they accelerated away and he ground to a halt, out of breath, angry, red-faced, fists clenching and unclenching.

He turned round and freewheeled back to the loch's edge, then carried on, expecting Kayla to appear around each bend as he retraced his route. The wind hummed in his ears, drowning out most other sounds apart from the omnipresent whirr of the chain and random bike squeaks.

Something was wrong. No idea what, but it nagged at his mind. Was it one of the phantom worries? It didn't feel like it, but they never did at the time. Always hard to know what you can believe.

She would have followed him eventually. No matter how annoyed she was.

He focussed on the road ahead, and reached the point where they'd stopped for food before he'd pissed off. He let his bike clatter against the bank and shouted her name, listened; nothing but the wind in the trees, birdsong, water trickling. Then he squatted by the wheel marks in the soft black mud, water pooling in the bottom. No curves indicated someone turning a bike around. It looked like she'd followed him, yet they hadn't passed. In that case, she must have turned off at some point. Why? Not the toilet again. Anger? No. Stopping to use his phone? Maybe. She could've seen a high point where a signal was likely, decided to climb it and ring ahead. If she'd still been down a side road or up a hill as he cycled past on his way here, then she could *now* be back on the main road, thinking she was catching up with him even though she just added to their distance. Shit.

He jumped on his bike and turned back towards Loch Duntelchaig again. He rode as fast as the first time, but now it was anxiety, not anger, that drove him. Each side road, track, drive or layby received a cursory glance. When programming he was always methodical, checking every subroutine, every line of code, squashing every bug. It saved errors and time in the long run.

One of the turn-offs did lead up a craggy hill. She might have gone there. He turned down the narrow lane. The sun-baked mud here was dry, impossible to tell if she'd come this way, but he could at least get to the highest point and look for a trace. It wouldn't waste much time, and if it was fruitless he could return to the Loch Duntelchaig road and hopefully catch up with her.

To his right was a field of shaggy cows, the kind Kayla called "Highland coos", all browns and reds, horned heads raised and staring at him with bovine laconic calmness through mop-like fringes. It was unnerving. You couldn't tell what they were thinking. Just big-eyed witnesses. Their lowing had a suffering quality that made him shudder.

He noticed a flash of artificial colour up ahead, beside some lichen-covered rocks that burst from the ground like misshapen warts. Stone and hardness everywhere in the Scottish Highlands. The colour disappeared as his angle changed, hidden by ferns, then he got another glimpse of whatever had attracted his eye as he neared. Something curved.

He reached the spot and braked.

It was her bike, lying among the ferns.

He let his own bike drop with a rattle like loose bones, shouting her name as he waded through the rustly undergrowth on foot. Huge black slugs twisted through the long damp grass by the cattle field. No reply. Just a stink of manure, rich and animal.

Her pannier was missing.

Flies buzzed around his head, crawled on his sweaty arm. He flicked them off and called again. Over a hedge he spotted rusting metal gates and a corrugated steel shed that had seen better days. The edge of a house in the distance. Another shout of her name. Unanswered. Then he spotted something on the verge about twenty feet ahead.

He rushed up to it and knelt. A tyre track had flattened plants and churned-up earth. Not a tractor, it was too small. Not a bicycle. Maybe not a car. Fresh, a huge fat slug half-squashed into the mud and leaking pale guts. The tyre mark followed a tight curve. The vehicle had been turning. It had gone back to the main road.

It couldn't be a coincidence. This wasn't paranoia, it was a gut feeling that was much stronger, screaming at him to act, to hurry, that precious time had slipped away while he floundered, slapping the ground in his futile fish-out-of-water shtick. Someone had needed him and he hadn't been there for her.

He patted the jacket pocket over his left breast but it was empty. Of course. She had *his* phone. So he couldn't ring her, or the police. He'd seen no payphones by the roads. Hell, you hardly saw them in the cities any more. Perhaps this lane was a drive leading to a farm eventually, but how long could that waste? What if –

The banging from the van.

He'd heard that. Interpreted as victorious crowing and taunting from the blokes.

But maybe it came from the rear of the van.

He snatched his bike and started back, pedalling fast even though it was downhill, braking at the last second to take the corner and head in the direction of Loch Duntelchaig, where the van had passed him – how long ago? Twenty minutes?

He would follow his instincts. To wherever they led him. This wasn't mindless, reactionary, selfish. This was for her.

I'm coming for you, Kayla.

HIS LEGS BURNED BUT HE didn't stop, just powered on, back soaking with sweat even though the sun had given up for a while and hidden behind misty grey sky. No vehicles passed him either way. No houses. Only these endless windy roads.

At the top of each rise he squinted ahead, looking for tell-tale signs of a white dot. Nothing. Too many bends. Too many copses of thick trees, and rough rock hills. But she'd come this way. He sensed it.

Then he reached a junction.

He couldn't remember which way their planned route would take them. He should have paid more attention. Not that it mattered if she wasn't in the driving seat. If she'd been kidnapped.

The turning to the right wound down, and led to a town, according to the sign, but it would take Ed at least an hour to get there. An hour too long. Left led on to a bridge over an expanse of water and a route that was more isolated. Probably fishing and hunting.

Maybe the blokes would avoid populated areas.

Left, then. The wind was blowing hard by the time he reached the low, totally exposed bridge, a squall churning huge waves over the loch so that the gusts which hit him side-on in unpredictable blasts also soaked him with carried water. He had to grit his teeth and lean sideways into the wind at about thirty degrees to avoid being blown over or smashed into the bridge's low barriers. It would be too easy to thwack against them and tumble over into the turbulent and icy waters below.

Kayla had grown up in this kind of wild place. What had she said about it? "Never be complacent." Something like that. He should have listened.

Even when the wind wasn't trying to kill him, it slowed his progress as if he dragged a huge cart behind rather than just an overloaded pannier. He should be used to it. He was always pulling that weight. Weight of the past. You can't get anywhere until you leave it behind. He knew that. They told him that. He suspected Kayla had been waiting for that.

And this was how he repaid her.

Grit blew in his face as he left the bridge, making his eyes smart. She'd also advised him to wear sunglasses. Again, he thought he'd known better.

Kayla.

Kayla Kayla Kayla.

He threw his head down and pumped the pedals even harder. All roads led somewhere. You just have to keep going, not give up.

ED WHIZZED ROUND ANOTHER DEAD-MAN'S curve blind and
hopeful rather than cautious and slow, which would waste time
getting back up to speed. The bike slid on a wet surface where
water trickled over the road as if the hill cried.

No oncoming traffic. No splat.

A long descent followed ... and then he saw houses up ahead.
A teeny settlement of higgledy-piggledy squat cottages on one
side of the road, and some kind of shop on the other. A group of
kids played football on a clumpy patch of grass to the side of the
end cottage.

But it was people.

It was help.

He flew onto the shop's forecourt and slammed on the brakes
at the last second, throwing him forward against the handlebars.
A sage-coloured Land Rover was parked there, plastered in mud
like a stock car. He ran his bike past and leaned it against the
fence. No time to waste getting the lock out.

Plant stalls lined the windows out front but he could see that
lights were on inside. He burst in through the front door, setting
a bell tinkling. It was a large general store. Newspapers by the
counter, shelves of bread and tinned soups, small freezers of meat
and chips. Firewood bundles, second-hand books.

He headed straight for the counter. The woman behind it was
in her sixties, with bleached blonde hair and bold eyeliner that
suggested she'd forgotten her age, and a muslin scarf tied round
her neck. She chatted to a middle-aged woman in wellies and a
waxed jacket, presumably the owner of the 4x4.

"It's been awful drych for the lambing," the shopkeeper said to her.

"I had to go round the fields in the Rover, catching them. Took the lambs to the kitchen to warm up while he put the others in pens –"

"Excuse me," interrupted Ed. "Are there any police near here?"

"Police?" asked the bleached blonde shopkeeper.

"Yes! I think my girlfriend's been kidnapped."

"Kidnapped?"

"Have you seen a white van? Today, or any time recently?"

A look passed between Granny Blondie and her sheepy friend. It could have been concern. Could just as easily be disbelief. Or something else. Recognition? "Well, you do get them, dearie," said the shopkeeper. "I can't recall any today, though."

She spoke so fucking slowly. Slowness of bucolic habit, or slowness of talking to someone you didn't believe?

"Look, I know it sounds bizarre but it's true. They might already be far away. I don't know the places round here, the roads. I need help!"

"Have you rung the police?" asked Land Rover Woman, frowning.

"No, my girlfriend had my phone. Can I use yours, please?"

The women looked at each other again.

Ed banged his fist on the counter. "It's fucking urgent!"

At that, Granny Blondie turned and headed towards the back of the shop, shuffling in a way that made him want to scream at her.

He grimaced at Land Rover Woman. Best he could do in terms of a reassuring smile. She didn't reciprocate, so he looked impatiently at the tourist tat instead, while waiting for the shop owner to come back. Curling leaflets of Scottish attractions. T-shirts in plastic that said "I SCOTLAND" or "Wanted: Nessie" while a stupid cartoon diplodocus wearing a tartan cap poked its head out of the waves.

Fuck!

He tapped his foot until she returned with a phone that trailed a long cord behind it, placing it on the counter in front of him. Both women watched while he dialled 999. Probably quicker than trying to find a number for the local police.

"Emergency. Which service?"

"Police."

"I'll just connect you now."

A pause, then:

"Police Service, where are you calling from?"

"Scotland. A shop. I don't know where, hold on." He rested the phone on his shoulder and got the shop owner to give him the address, which he repeated line by line.

"What is the nature of your emergency? Tell me exactly what's happened."

"I think my girlfriend's been kidnapped. By some thugs in a white van. They could be anywhere by now, I need you to get people out here and search, close roads or something!" He noticed his voice rising.

"Please, take a deep breath. I'm making a note of everything and can pass details on while you are speaking, but I need to know those details first."

He hated people telling him to keep calm, being superior to him, digging at him. "I was out cycling with my girlfriend near here. She's Kayla Dean. A white van like a transit went past with blokes in, and they – yes, she's twenty-seven, five ten, brown hair, shoulder-length, dressed in purple leggings, new pink trainers, cycling top – that's mauve, or blue, or cyan, I don't know! – and the blokes acted aggressively then drove off. Me and my girlfriend got split up temporarily, and when I went back –" tyres crunching on gravel as another customer arrived for their oatcakes and milk "– she was gone but her bike was in the bushes. No, it was just after the van had gone past again, and –" a quick glance out, then a double take as the door to the van opened and the bloke with a beanie and stuck-out ears dropped to the forecourt. "Shit, they're here!" he hissed. "Stay on the line!" He rested the phone on the counter.

"That's the van, the kidnappers," he explained to the two women, who glanced slack-jawed from him to the van. Ed ducked behind the counter without asking – the wooden counter flap had been leaning against the wall at an angle. He was now out of sight. Thinking.

They didn't know he was here.

His bicycle – no, they wouldn't have seen it on the other side of the Land Rover.

If they spotted him, they'd drive off. Game over.

If he went out the front they'd drive off. Game over.

Maybe he could wait until the guy came in, try and overpower him, but it could go wrong so easily.

Police were on the line. They'd listen, that was good, best to buy time, keep the van here as long as possible.

If Ed could somehow get to the van unseen he might be able to disable it, or open the rear door, or stop the beanie guy from returning to it.

"Do you have a back route I can go out? I need to check that van for my girlfriend without them seeing me!" he asked in a rush. The shopkeeper nodded and led the way through the doorway she'd fetched the phone from. It was a small hall with a room to the side and a door at the end, frosted glass showing a compound-eye vision of green and grey. Exterior. He rushed ahead of her towards it. A tinkle from the shop as someone entered. Ed yanked at the back door. Twice. It was locked. He spotted a catch and a bolt, opened it quietly as possible.

"Go back, act natural, hopefully the police will come," he whispered to the woman, who seemed unable to speak. An ornament on a wooden bureau held down a stack of papers. He snatched it up. A weighty glass globe encasing a sea urchin. The woman flinched, but he held a finger to his lips, "Shhh!" then slipped out the back, letting the door close behind him and muffling the Scottish accents that indicated talk in the shop.

Ed moved along the side of the building then peeped round the corner. The back of the van faced him, but it was fifteen metres away. He'd have to hope the driver didn't glance in his wing mirror during the dash. Ed would also be in full view if the guy in the shop looked out at the forecourt. Couldn't be helped.

Ed crouch-ran across the open space. His head was below the height of the for-sale plants. So far so good. No shouts. He squatted at the back of the van. Dirty. Not just city grime, the kind kids would finger-write "Clean me!" in, but proper mud, behind the wheels, at the base. It had been off-road sometime. He couldn't remember if it had been so plastered in crap earlier.

It was a double door at the back. The silvery handle had a button you depressed before turning it, Yale-type lock in the centre. It would make noise, but he could try that, throw open the door. He peeped round the side of the van first. It hadn't been looked after well. Scratches. Minor dents. One of them, a black streak, at a bicycle's handlebar height.

A peek at the shop. Beanie Man was talking with the shopkeeper and her friend. Agitated. Gesturing. One of the women pointed towards the front of the shop. It could have meant anything but the guy happened to glance that way and saw Ed looking back at him. Eyes locked, no mistaking the recognition. The guy ran towards the shop's entrance. Ed grabbed the van's back door handle, pushed his thumb in but the button didn't depress. He tried turning the handle anyway, hard as he could, but it was locked tight. He pounded on the van with his fist, shouting "KAYLA, ARE YOU IN THERE? KAYLA!" as the man from the shop bowled into him, sending him sprawling in the dust, the heavy paperweight rolling away. Ed snatched it as the bloke kicked him, catching him a good one in the ribs, but Ed scrambled up now, held the paperweight high, threatening, advancing on the bloke.

"Let me in the van," Ed said.

"Drop yer chuckie stane, ye heider," Beanie Man replied, staring at the paperweight.

The clunk of a vehicle door opening. Another one of them getting out?

Suddenly Beanie sprinted out of sight. Ed followed but he was already climbing into the van, pulling the door closed behind him as the engine started up, farting diesel smoke. He ran towards the door and grabbed the handle but the lock stud had already been depressed. Three blokes in the front. The middle one had a bald head and flattened nose; he stared into Ed's eyes as the van roared off, just missing running over his feet. Ed smashed at one of the rear lights as it passed, shattering it, but also smashing the paper weight into shards. He dropped the pieces and ran after the van for a few steps. No good, it had already careered onto the road. His hand stung, blood trickling down the palm and dripping onto the ground.

The broken light might help identify the van.

He rushed to his bike, took off the pannier. Its weight would only slow him down. He removed one item from it, slipped it into a pocket, then opened the shop door. The two women stared at him, slack-jawed. The phone's receiver had been replaced. Any help from them would be slow. Slow was no good. He couldn't risk losing her.

"Phone the police back," he shouted at the shopkeeper. "Tell them what happened. I'm going after them. Broke a tail-light on the van. I'll leave this here." He threw his pannier inside the shop, letting it scuff along the floor for a metre.

There was something wrong in the way she looked at him. But no time to ponder it now.

He sprinted back to his bike, leapt on, and started after the van.

THEY'D TAKEN A DIFFERENT ROUTE from the windy bridge. Uphill. But not just a hill. It was one of those hills that reach up into the sky, disappearing into misty grey wetness. Oh joy of fucking joys.

Teeth gritted, he stood, hammering down on each revolution to make as much progress as possible, slow motion pedalling through treacle. He had to do it. Every second his distance from Kayla grew.

It had clouded over and the ground dotted with rain. He lowered his head, gripped the handlebars tight. The right one was sticky with blood, a tearing sucking sensation every time he moved that hand, but the throbbing pain was good, distracted him from the agony elsewhere: the burning in his quads, the aches in his knees, the tightness in the muscles of his groin, the bruising of his sitting bones and the soreness of arms held tense in one position for so long. He never wanted to get on a bike again.

To distract himself he thought about something Kayla had said. About gear changes. It came back to him now, stuff he'd barely paid attention to at the time. "Always get into a gear where you can sing Twinkle Twinkle Little Star as your legs go round." That was it. If you sang too fast, go up a gear; if too slow, down a gear. She knew so much. He'd taken it for granted.

"Twin-kle-twin-kle-litt-le-star."

He wanted her like never before. He had to tell her. Tell her how he felt.

"How-I-won-der-what-you-are."

This made no sense. That a day could begin so nice, and turn into *this*. But the world had also turned upside down in another way. He would rescue *her* for once, whatever it took. He was being a man. It was what she'd secretly wanted. Needed. He should have listened sooner. Should have listened to a lot of things.

No sight of the van ahead but it must be there somewhere. He'd catch up if it stopped. He'd ask for more help if he came across any. Maybe the van would break down. Or maybe the police would turn up first. He was doing the right thing. Catch up with the bastards. Catch up for Kayla.

"Up-a-bove-the-world-so-high."

Mud and water washed down the road towards him, gluey ebbs slowing him even more. He had to go through it. Push on.

"Like-a-di-amond-in-the-sky."

The hardest material. By the side of the road mossy rocks resembled curled-up lumpy beasts, asleep so long the green stretched a blanket over their irregular forms. He would like to sleep for a hundred years as well.

"As-your-bright-and-ti-ny-spark."

A darkness to the grey ahead. Top of the hill? His breath came in ragged gasps, pulling in cold air, icy moisture.

"Lights-the-trav-eller-in-the-dark."

The roads didn't seem like they belonged. Laid on uncertain foundations. The edges of the tarmac were cracked, crumbled into the ditches. The ground wanted to reclaim things, take them back to the wild state it had never forgotten.

"Though-I-know-not-what-you-are."

And he did know, now. They were wrong. All those who said he was paranoid. No, he was right all along. Justified in his choices when going into the wilds. Good that he'd kept a folding knife in the pannier. Its weight now reassured him.

If it hadn't been pouring with rain there would have been excellent views. Wild views. The isolated highlands – he finally understood them. Was part of them. And laughed. He laughed and laughed. Pain didn't bother him. It might make him scream, and if he screamed he might not stop, but for now it was grounding, pure. Pain didn't let you down. Maybe Kayla was in pain, and he'd deserve to feel it a hundred times over. It was his fault. His fucking fault. And still he laughed, because he was afraid to stop.

"Twin-kle-twin-kle-litt-le-star."

And that star was Kayla.

He'd done it. The road finally levelled out. Higher, and more exposed, weather getting worse. The sky was like the murky bottom of dirty icebergs floating over the washed-out greyness above as sheets of blasting rain gusted over the uplands. The few trees up here were grown bent by a lifetime of the wind's force, twisted like a painful deformity or an old man's spine. But they endured. He could appreciate that. He and Kayla would endure. Yes.

But, like the trees, it was difficult to keep straight. Water dripped from his nose and the peak of his cycle helmet. It somehow got down the back of his neck too. Just keep going. He squinted to focus on the road and whatever was beyond. For any sign of the van.

There. In a pause in the curtain of rain. Something greyish and small. Maybe a distant sheep ... or an even more distant vehicle. He ignored the next few side roads, then turned off in the direction of the phantom shape. Grateful to notice it was a steep downhill. He freewheeled, standing to rest some of the arse aches but keeping his fingers on the brakes, feathering them to retain a feeling of control on the slippery road. Under other circumstances the descent might be fun and exhilarating, a long straight with good advance warning of oncoming traffic, but today it was just scary. An accident here would be serious.

Off to one side the hills dropped away, down to the flat grey of a loch, choppy in the wind but still reflecting the mountains beyond in broken spikes. A road down there circled the body of water, with woods off to one side.

And just for a second: tail-lights. Glowing red like a pair of eyes drifting in the mist.

Gone. But the steep hairpin bends cutting the hillside meant he could get down there a lot quicker than he'd got up. He kicked off and continued his descent, fast, too fast, the bike wobbled when he braked, the back wheel skidding left and right. He shook his head to try and clear water from his face so he could see better, but it was useless. Clothes soaked now. The skin in his palm split apart again as he had to twist and bank sharply after hitting a water-filled pothole. Every time he faced towards where he'd seen the lights he squinted for another glance, but nothing. View blocked by trees as he got lower. At least at the bottom he'd be on the flat, could hammer it to get to that point. He licked his lips, taking in refreshing moisture for his parched mouth. Another sharp turn, nearly there, wind in his ears, freezing them and reducing sound to just that drone above spinning wheels; a final lean round a particularly sharp bend and he could guide the bike onto the flat at good speed ... straight into blinding high-beam headlights, followed by the grinding crunch of impact.

HE WAS FLYING. WEIGHTLESS. IT was liberating.

For a second.

Then his groin was brutally bashed by part of the bike, body twisting, followed by a hard thwack and crunch that must have been head meeting pavement.

Once he stopped tumbling he stared up at the sky. The rain fell into his eyes, silver spears in the headlights, pummelling him. Blood in his mouth. He ran a tongue around. Something hard. Chipped tooth. He turned his head to the side and spat it out. His neck protested. His head protested. His whole fucking body protested, though he supposed head and neck were the vital ones that determined how fucked he was.

A car door opening, footsteps coming closer. Ed sat up, risking further damage if he had a broken neck or spine. He reached for his knife but his arm had been pinned behind him. No feeling in it. Possibly something torn. He got ready to fight.

"Oh God, are ye all right, man?"

Sounded Scottish but concerned. Ed didn't think it was the van that had hit him. He flopped back and groaned.

"Is my head still attached?"

"Just about. You came out of nowhere, ye fuckin eejit!"

"Help me up."

"No way. Ye could be broken."

"I'm in a hurry. Least you can do after knocking me down."

The man grumbled but helped Ed to stand. Pain raged down on him like the weather. Ed blinked water out of his eyes to see the bloke more clearly: wavy hair already sopping, tweedy jacket darkening. In his fifties, a grey-flecked but trimmed beard. Ed reached to the back of his head, felt a massive lump, almost panicked before recognising the cycle helmet. It was loose, broken somehow, but it might have saved his life. Thanks to Kayla's nagging.

Kayla.

Ed's cargo pants were ripped. He was sure bruises covered his wrecked body by now. At least he'd stopped laughing.

"Aren't you meant to slow at a junction?" Ed asked.

"You're one to talk, laddie."

"I got reasons."

"Save them for later. You okay? Can ye walk?"

The car's engine was running, a chugging vibration behind all other sounds. The front lights turned sleety rain into sparklers.

Ed took a step, unaided, and his legs didn't buckle as he'd expected. Slow, but possible.

The man opened the passenger-side door. "Get in, oot of the rain. I'll see if I can put your bike in the boot then get you to a hospital. A bit of a drive but Raigmore is closest."

Ed hobbled over and climbed into the passenger seat. The deluge thrummed on the roof instead of his head, but he was so soaked it made little difference now.

The man walked over to the bicycle, illuminated as if in spotlights, then lifted it up so Ed could see. The front wheel was buckled, chain hanging off. Busted, probably too big for the boot.

Ed was thinking again as the shock of impact faded. This was all wasting time. If he went to hospital it would be too late to do anything then. And for Kayla he would do anything. *Anything.*

The keys were in the ignition.

Ed pressed the lock down on the door, then slid over the gear stick into the driving seat and did the same there.

The driver saw what he was doing and ran to the car, pulled the handle in vain, banged on the glass. Ed lowered it an inch by turning the manual handle. Didn't see those any more.

"What the feck are ye doin?"

"My girlfriend's been kidnapped. Sorry to leave you in the rain, but get the police. Send them after me."

"I'll get the police all right, yer a fuckin loony with yer head knocked!"

The man moved in front of the car and planted his hands on the bonnet to stop Ed advancing.

Ed didn't want to go forwards anyway. He put it in reverse, backed away quickly so the man stumbled forward. Ed turned in the seat to check behind, such poor visibility, and his neck objected as if it had bolts through it. Fuck. But he kept going, the engine whining in that weird pitch you only hear in fast reverse.

Once he'd left the bloke far enough behind he did a three-point-turn at a layby and headed off. This was good. He could catch them now, maybe. If not, the police would soon be after them all.

THIS TIME HE COULD TAKE the high roads without exhausting himself. Just as well, since he had aches on top of aches, and a layer of pain on top of that – some sharp, and some throbbing, for variety. He kept his head thrust forward. The seat was luxury after sitting on a torturous wedge for so long.

The rain eased to drizzle. He turned off the windscreen wipers, their rubbery squeals ceasing so he could hear better. Road signs pointed to settlements but if the van went that way it would be found by the police eventually – there were bound to be cameras there. Whereas if they stayed in the wilds they'd be more likely to get outside of a search radius without detection. Best to spend his limited time here.

The glove box contained an A-To-Z, small binoculars and a half packet of mints. While driving he opened the A-To-Z on the seat next to him with one hand. He worked out where he was from the last two signposts and realised he'd been following a route that skirted lochs and farms. That felt right somehow. Maybe his instinct was on to something.

At the next high point he parked at the edge of a steep drop and got out. Long husky grasses rolled in silvered waves as the angry wind tousled it. He checked the mud for van-like tyre tracks. Inconclusive. Then he scrambled up onto the car's roof, slippery with moisture, and turned slowly, surveying the scene, checking for movement on any of the roads. He focussed the binoculars on anything that seemed promising. One car. One church. One deer. No van.

Some birds taking off attracted his eye. From woods much lower down. A mile or so away. Then they were gone. He zoomed in anyway. Nothing. Except a sound. Faint, but he realised he'd heard it while he was turning. Thought it was his trainers squeaking on the car roof, but it happened again – a mild thud, more like a distant car backfiring. Hard to tell the direction for sure, the way sounds echoed up here, pinballing between surfaces, but probably where the birds took off. Once more. Not a backfire. More like gunfire.

He had nothing else to go on so slid down the bonnet on his arse, clambered into the car, threw the binoculars down, scanned the map and identified the quickest way there. A dead-end road leading into some kind of Forestry Commission land. Maybe a dead end in other ways. He took off, pressed back into the seat by acceleration.

A BATTERED SIGN HUNG ASKEW at the turn off.

"No shooting. No trespassers. Private."

Parallel muddy ruts led under the cover of pines, grass growing up in the centre. The long gate was wedged open. He slowed when he saw something shine on the floor like a coiled snake. Lowered his window and stuck his head out to look. A chain with a padlock. It had been cut rather than unlocked. That would require bolt-cutters. A toolbox. A big vehicle to transport them in. He rolled forward, passing through a wide clearing with damp logs stacked up in an elongated prism.

Then it was dark again, the trees crowding in tight, creating a thick canopy where the only thing that grew was an ever-deepening bed of orange-brown needles. The car jostled and bumped as the rough track curved, sometimes scraping the underneath. Damage, maybe. There would be all sorts of costs and implications from this day.

There. A vehicle parked ahead, in another widening stretch. Dirty white van, back door ajar. Young bloke in a black jacket talking to a bald guy in camo gear. And the third – it was the guy with stuck-out ears and a beanie. He held a shotgun over one arm, breached open, doing something to it. Another shotgun leaned against the van next to him. He glanced up at the car. Suspicion in his eyes, but he didn't know who was behind the wheel. Not yet.

Black jacket looked up, then closed the rear van door quickly. Guiltily. As he moved Ed could see the camo-coated bloke putting down a spade just out of sight in a subtle but shifty movement.

Ed put the seatbelt on. He hadn't bothered with it up until now. It clicked into place. He edged the car left, as if to go around the van, then suddenly accelerated and swerved right. The big-eared beanie bloke with the gun had nowhere to go, was smashed from the car's bonnet, broken, a look of surprise on his face. A bump, and a second bump as the wheels crushed him, then the

149

car crunched into the flank of the van, thrusting it to the side and slamming to a halt. Ed's head flew forwards and hit the steering wheel, unfortunately connecting with his face rather than the cycle helmet. Whiplash pain spasmed down his spine but he leaned back and undid the seatbelt as it slackened, clambered over the passenger seat and out that door, falling to the mud on his elbows. Shouts and swearing from behind his car. Maybe they could see part of their mate stuck out from under a wheel. Hopefully the guns were under there too and not accessible. Ed used the car door to stand, bit down on tearing agony in his neck.

"The fuck?" said the young guy with the black jacket. Noises in the van. Scrabbling.

Bald camo guy had the spade again, swung it at Ed, who ducked but too late, his reflexes slowed – a hefty part of it clunked against his shoulder and head, sending him sprawling. This time the cycle helmet finally gave up the ghost and broke in two, the straps digging into his neck and choking him. Grey polystyrene where it split, but better than seeing the grey matter between his ears if his head had been unprotected. He yanked it off and threw it away as the guy swung again, but Ed was low and rolled to the side so the spade bounced off the car door with a comedy clang, scraping a huge chunk of paintwork in the process. Ed grabbed onto the spade before it could be pulled back again, tucked it under his left arm and tried to clamp it in place, but the bald guy was too strong for that and yanked, determined to get the spade back. Ed was dragged along the ground, he'd never win this tug of war but it didn't matter, it was temporary, because his free hand, the one he'd sliced open earlier, reached into his pocket and took a grip on the handle there. His thumb found the stud and released the blade with a smooth practised rotation. It clicked into the locked position, a few inches of hard and incredibly sharp steel. Only as the spade yanked him closer again did he pull it out and thrust upwards from his low position, aiming at anywhere near the guy's stomach but not being able to reach that high – the knife plunged into the flesh near the top of his thigh, puncturing almost to the handle so that the blade made a grisly scraping sound across bone at a nasty upward angle. The bloke dropped the spade immediately and fell on his back, blood pumping from his inner thigh in a sickening bright red squirt, soaking his hands as he tried to clamp them over the wound.

Paydirt: must be an artery. He wouldn't be getting up in a hurry.

Ed turned on what he hoped was the last of them, the one in the black jacket. He looked the youngest, about sixteen. Instead of attacking he seemed to be in a daze, mouth open at what had happened. Lasted seconds, felt like years, something like that.

No sounds from under the car, but Ed saw a mangled leg stuck out. Good. Safe.

Another noise from in the van. Frantic scraping. A high-pitched whine.

"Where is she?" Ed asked, advancing with a limp. He'd have no chance of catching the lad if he got too scared and ran. "I just want to talk," Ed said, as calmly as he could. "Answer my questions and it will be fine."

"It's ye!" said the lad, recognition finally dawning on his sparsely whiskered face.

"It's me."

"We're sorry about your girlfriend," the lad said. "Honest. Shouldnae ha done it. Would take it back if ah could."

At last, they'd admitted it. Ed had been right all along. He reached out for the lad's shoulder, intending to grab a fistful of jacket, but Ed but was too slow. The lad turned and hightailed it towards the trees. Ed slipped the knife into his pocket, reached down between the car and van, fumbled round and touched the tip of one of the guns, dragged it forward until he could pick it up. It was the one that had leaned against the van. He stared at it for a second as the lad scrambled up a slope, digging out clumps of pine needles in his panicked ascent, and Ed realised it was too late. He wasn't sure how to fire a gun, or check if it was loaded – did they have safety switches or something? And he doubted he'd pull off that shot on his first ever attempt. Fuck. He lay the gun on the floor instead. As he did so he noticed what looked like a bloodstain on the van's rear bumper. Had that been there before? The noises from in the van didn't sound like a person any more. Animal sounds. They'd moved her. Somewhere in the trees.

The lad was out of sight now, no doubt running for his life. But the bald bloke Ed had stabbed still tried to wriggle away on his back like a worm that had been chopped in half by a spade. Ed approached him. Baldie tried to move faster but the unstabbed leg kept slipping on the wet grass. The camo trousers were stained cherry with blood.

"Ye fucker," Baldie said, between gritted teeth, trying to keep hands clamped on the pulsing wound.

Ed knelt.

"Where is she?"

"Havnae got the besom."

Ed gripped the guy's wrists and removed his hands from the leg wound. The bloke tried to resist but was too weak. Crimson fluids still gushed. The ground was spilled with gore. It didn't sicken Ed. It was justice.

"You'll die if I don't get you an ambulance."

"There's a phone in ma pocket."

"Good. Where did you leave her?"

A grimace, then resignation in that hard face. "Way back." He jutted his chin towards a point off in the woods maybe, vague and useless. The shovel still lay on the floor nearby. Ed could see fresh dirt on it. He took the knife from his pocket and tried to stab the guy in the throat. They tussled on the floor, Ed had to lie on top of him and use both hands, but the knife tip edged towards the man's neck, pinched the skin, "No!" said the guy but Ed leaned harder and saw the blade plunge beneath the flesh, sliding in with no more resistance and immediately spurting a red geyser into Ed's face and chest. Ed rolled off and away, leaving the knife embedded. The guy was bucking but wouldn't be getting up again.

Ed immediately regretted it.

He'd killed him too quickly.

Same with the one he'd run over. Maybe he could catch the lad, make him show where they'd taken her. What had they done? Was there a chance she was still alive?

He stood shakily, made his way to the van, and promptly fell against it, causing growls from inside. Weaker by the minute as the adrenaline faded, letting hopelessness slip inside in its place, like darkness filling a hollow. Cold as the water at the bottom of a loch.

He grasped the handle, turned it, and yanked.

The smell. Blood and shit. Two dogs barked at him from the cage built into the van. Some kind of large terriers. More spades, an empty sack, and a big tub that contained black and white fur. No, it was a dead animal. More than one. Looked like badgers, but torn apart, bite marks in the raw wounds that still leaked.

Ed slammed the door closed, muffling the angry hounds. Back to Baldie with the knife handle still stuck out of his neck. He'd stopped moving, stopped squirting blood everywhere. Ed rummaged in the bloke's camo jacket pockets until he found the phone. He could call the police. They'd get the location from GPS, maybe. But that could be too late.

Wherever she was, they might have left Ed's phone on her body. He could dial his *own* number. Listen out for it. Go and wander round the woods while it rang. There might still be time.

The camo guy's phone was an old one. Buttons for numbers. It wasn't locked. Ed paced as he dialled with one blood-slick hand, leaving red smudges across the surface.

It rang. It rang. He didn't expect an answer, instead looking around, trying to hear its echo from nearby. He nearly dropped the phone when it clicked and a voice spoke to him.

"Hello? Who's this?" she asked.

At first he couldn't reply.

"If you don't speak I'm hanging up."

Ed fell to his knees, gripping the phone tight. Sniffed hard, because suddenly it felt like his head was filling up with water.

"Kayla. It's me," he said, hoarsely.

"About fucking time, you bastard."

"Kayla? I've been out looking for you ... are you okay?"

"No thanks to you. I got knocked off my bike! And they did it on purpose, I'm sure of it. Probably because of your stupid bullshit."

"Where are you?"

"At the farm still. I walked here after they drove off. The farmer and his wife looked after me, and the police are here. Where are you? I've overheard some weird stuff."

"You don't know what ..." But he had to stop, wipe his nose on the back of a bloody hand, take deep breaths to continue. "What I've been through."

"How dare you say that!" She was shouting. "How dare you! After you fucked off in another of your moods ... it wouldn't have happened if you'd stayed with me! But that's you all over. So fucking selfish. I don't care about your problems, your excuses. You know what? It's over, Ed. I can't take it any more. Where the fuck are you anyway? I think the police are –"

He pressed end call. Slumped to the floor, leaning against the back of the van. When he looked down he saw he was covered in gore. Like something from a horror film. His face was tight with it as it crusted and flaked. He glanced at his reflection in the small square of the phone's display but didn't recognise himself. So he started laughing again. The phone dropped in the mud.

What goes up must go down. That was the rule. He eyed the shotgun to his side. Twinkle twinkle, little star. There was time. To wait. And think. And decide what came next.

FileKiller

TRINA PEELED BACK THE TISSUE paper and inhaled fresh plastic, canvas, chemical cleanness. She trapped the scent in her lungs. 3mm negative soles. She would be the fastest.

They must stay enclosed and perfect until the first trial. A glance revealed the shelves were packed. Bottom drawer then. But that was also crammed. Lives so full cannot be sentimental. She lifted the first box of photos. "1991" it said in cracked glitter pen. She knew the contents. Labels save looking. Running shoes in one hand, memories trapped in red-speckled amber on the other. She weighed them up, then dropped the box of photos into the steel bin; they clanged, hollow, the echo faded because everything fades. Sound is a dead thing. By the time you hear, it's already over.

The trainers were neatly placed in their perfect space. The drawer closed smoothly.

THAT NIGHT WAS A DATE. Mezze.

"Good choice," Malcolm said. "I like sharing."

She smiled. That wasn't the reason. No dish overstays its welcome.

"What's your favourite thing to do?" he asked. The glint in his eye reminded her of olive oil.

"Winning," she said.

LATER. HE GOT DRESSED IN silence.

Every man is ninety per cent disappointment.

MAYBE SHE SHOULD HAVE SAID running was her favourite thing, she thought, while pounding down the canal-side path to work the next day, breaking in the new shoes.

Running. A lie? Her favourite thing, yes. But she hated it too.

It was a means to an end. Like people. Like possessions. You have to have them. You have to do it. You have to play the game to fit in, to be a good girl. And she was fucking good. Playing the game is pointless unless you win.

She ran faster, feet heavy but bouncing back with every step, using the world's hardness to get ahead. Never give up. She overtook the person in front and kept going, breathless but smiling with lungs burning tight.

KNUCKLES RAPPED ON THE OFFICE door frame. "Hey you," Malcolm said, distracting her from her screen.

She turned the display off and faced him. He looked better with clothes on. Without smart outfits men were just dangle bits and hangups.

"What?" she asked, frowning at the interruption.

"I just wanted to say thanks for last night."

"No problem."

"Fancy going out again tonight? Since it's a Friday there's no need to get up early tomorrow. I like to lounge in –"

"I'm going to be busy this weekend, unfortunately."

"Oh."

Maybe he was waiting for her to speak. Damned if she would.

After a pause he added, "You look great today. Your hair, your ..." But he lost it. The cockiness. It was easy to manipulate people to the outcome you wanted when their emotional impulses and egos were so predictable.

"Really," she said. "Thank you."

During another awkward silence his smile completely evaporated. "I like the idea of us," he said. "We're heads of the two biggest departments. It makes sense. And yet you're the only person I know who can make 'thank you' sound like 'fuck you'."

The way he was looking at her: at first expecting a reaction to what he thought was a joke; then realising that he'd hit the nail on the head and the spark was both imaginary and dead. Just to make sure there was a zero per cent chance of it ever catching fire again, it needed grinding under her heel.

"I tweaked and submitted my draft proposals for the next financial this morning," she said, tapping her blank screen but holding his gaze. "It's being considered at the moment. The plan would need the IT budget as well as a chunk of provisional spend. I showed that it was possible."

"But that would mean we couldn't do my projects! We need a new CMS and training and – oh. I told you about my ideas. Last night."

"Sorry, Malcolm. I always win." She held thumb and forefinger to her forehead in a letter L. One zap of the Loser symbol was all it took for him to storm off.

Men. Ninety per cent disappointment. But ten per cent useful.

"YES. I'LL WORK ON IT this weekend."

She hung up and savoured the buzz, the relief, tighten/relax, opposites co-existing, fighting for dominance, just like hate and love.

The CEO confirmed that she had it. It was clear. Her report was the best.

She packed her bag to go home and was locking up her office when Eduardo appeared with his usual wide smile. A programmer from another department who was seconded to hers for one day a week, and an occasional running companion.

"No training tonight?" he asked.

"Taking a car from the pool. Somewhere I need to go on the way home."

"Ah. Well, I got something for you." He held out a USB stick.

"What is it?"

"A challenge doing the rounds. FileKiller."

She took the USB stick off him but said nothing.

"It's a ... game. Sort of," he explained. "One that scans the files on your hard drive. Deletes one at random if you play and only tells you what the file was after you click continue. To win you have to go through twenty rounds."

"Deleted to the recycle bin?"

"Nope. Deleted forever. There's no going back. Not if you want to win."

"That's not a game. It's malware with a win condition."

"I know!" He laughed. "No one should be psycho enough to play it. But they do. Just like they played Lose/Lose, which had an online high score table based on how many files people destroyed."

"Have you played it?"

"I ... no. Not got past the first screen. Couldn't go through with it. I thought about running it in a virtual environment, or moving off my personal files first, but that defeats the point, doesn't it? So I just closed it again. And yet ... now I know it's there ... it exists and I could run it ..." He stared at the USB stick she'd taken. "It scares me that I *might*. So I thought maybe passing it on will take away the temptation. And I know how you like to win. I'm still aching from running with you the other day. If anyone could do it, you could." He stared at her for a second too long. A challenge? No, it was ...

"Did Malcolm send you?"

The smile faded and Eduardo looked down, and nodded. "I mentioned it to him yesterday; just now he told me to show you. He said for once you'd lose. And actually, I hope he's right. Who'd want to win at this?"

"Did he play it?"

That brought energy back to Eduardo's face. "Ha, no! He's definitely too scared. Made an excuse about security, but I know that look. Maybe I should just do one level, so I can be better than my boss."

"Mmm." She slipped the USB stick in her bag. "But Eduardo, don't ever be his lapdog again. You'd be on the losing team."

SHE MADE A STOP-OFF ON the way home.

"Everything's going well, Dad."

He was collapsed in on himself, no *power* any longer, could hardly even see hers through distortedly thick lenses. In turn, she burnt all the brighter, the only star that existed in the solar system of burnt-out husks in an expensive nursing home. Her very existence was a taunt, and that was good.

"I knew it would." He smiled. Still had good teeth. Then, before she realised what was happening, he caressed her forearm with a liver-spotted hand, said, "You're a good girl, Trina." She flinched and withdrew, sick.

"Don't!" she said between clenched teeth, air tight in her lungs; it was called a rib cage for a reason.

Ice cream. Holidays. Sitting on knees. Tissue paper presents. Nice dresses. Long socks. Bedtime stories.

Opposites fighting. Disgust won.

"You don't. Ever."

SHE CURLED UP ON HER bed with a laptop, skimming Facebook, cocooned in pillows and blankets: her internest. But it was as boring as usual. All sorts of people asked to be her friend on social media. She normally clicked yes, left it a few weeks, then deleted them. They never noticed. If you lost touch with someone it was for a reason, they shouldn't keep reappearing like bad smells. More than three friends was just extravagance anyway.

The final proposal for the board was almost complete. She'd add a sprinkle of unnecessary graphs, because the section head liked them. Tools to convince the simple with pretty lights and colours. She could finish it later, or tomorrow. Another hour would put it to bed. After the phone call earlier she had no doubt they'd go along with what she suggested. Persuading people was too easy. She yawned and reached for her coffee from the bedside table. The coffee was cold. She finished it anyway. Like food, it was just fuel for the body, keeping the machine efficient.

She put the cup back but it refused to sit flat. She lifted it and saw she had placed it on the USB stick. It stood out as an 8GB stranger on the otherwise tidy bedside table. "FileKiller". Such a stupid idea.

She went back to her laptop, scrolling endlessly, but couldn't focus. She'd been rubbing her forearm, as if removing a spot of dirt. Idle fingers and devils. She stretched over and picked up the USB stick. Such small and beautiful things, yet tough and capable of holding a huge amount of depth. She was about to slip it into a USB port, because that's where they go, sticks in slots, when something cautioned her.

IT people. Hmmm.

Instead she used her browser to check if FileKiller existed. It did. She found a page with the original files and read the description.

> *The game selects 20 files from your computer at random*
>
> *to win, you must delete them all*
>
> *you don't know what each file is until AFTER you've deleted it.*
>
> *files 10 and 20 are folders, deleting them deletes everything in them*
>
> *there is no undo*
>
> *this game is real, and yes, it could seriously fuck up your computer/work/job/life.*

She downloaded a zip file to her desktop, then opened it. The folder contained FileKiller.exe and README.txt. She opened the readme out of curiosity. It only contained two lines.

THIS GAME IS DANGEROUS.

DO NOT PLAY IT!

It sounded like something a parent would tell you. "Don't pick things up off the floor." "Don't talk to the smelly kid in school." "Don't eat all your chocolates in one go."

Fuck that. She double-clicked on the .exe file.

A black screen with white text opened. That colour scheme made it seem even more serious. There was a repeat of the warnings and a recap of the rules. You could quit at any time with the Escape key.

Nothing would happen yet. She read the text twice to be sure.

She clicked on "I know the risks, I accept all responsibility for playing". Just to see.

The screen refreshed.

#1/20 - Random File

There is no going back if you delete this file,

it could be any file that is on your computer...

...but then to win, you must delete it. play, or give up (Escape key)

CLICK TO DELETE FILE

A row of paper sheets, portrayed by icons, each displayed a red question mark. The first one was highlighted with a glow, and rotated slowly.

It was waiting.

Waiting.

Waiting.

She only needed to delete a single file and she would beat Malcolm and all his department.

It rotated.

One file. One click.

It might be an important file.

But that was the point, wasn't it? The risk. What you put on the line in order to win. There was always a cost. Otherwise it meant nothing. But that cost needn't be one she couldn't bear.

The waiting was the worst thing.

She clicked on the button.

The first icon changed to an image of ripped up paper.

A message appeared at the bottom of the screen.

DELETED: C:\Program Files\Windows Journal\ Templates\Dotted_Line.jtp

She'd been holding her breath. She let it out.

Dotted_Line.jtp didn't seem like an important file. She didn't even recognise the programme. Huh. She'd won, and it was so easy it didn't even feel like she'd earned it.

The screen had moved to the next icon, instructions repeated below "#2/20 - Random File".

She could quit now. But what if someone in Malcom's team also deleted a file? Eduardo might do it over the weekend. The biggest milestone was deleting *one*. Most people would stop there. If you deleted two, you were far less likely to get superseded.

Fine. She clicked DELETE.

DELETED: D:\historical\2014\note.jpg

What was that? She couldn't even picture it. A scanned note, or a photo of one? It can't have been important if she couldn't even remember what it was or why she'd kept it. That meant its deletion was a good thing. Tidying up her hard drive. So much crud gathered if you weren't strict with it. Things you would never look at again. Never need.

She pressed the Print Screen button on her keyboard. She could paste it into an email to Eduardo and Malcolm. She'd deleted two out of twenty. It was important that they saw what she'd achieved.

She was about to open the email program when she realised that if she sent that image, they'd be tempted to beat her. Two files didn't seem much. They could do that in seconds. Knowing the way the clowns in IT behaved, they would make their victory score the department's desktop background for a day. Probably put it on her work PC too, just to rub her nose in it. "A puny two out of twenty? I scored THREE!"

Bastards.

Fine. One more.

DELETED: C:\Users\Trina\Desktop\changelist.docx

Ha, that was ... mmm. She'd saved that file as something to skim through for the next meeting. Still, it wasn't a major thing. In fact, it saved her time doing an unimportant job. She could devote that time to something better. This was ... well, almost fun.

Anyway, she'd done it. Faced the worst and won. She could press Escape and finish her report.

Though if she pressed Escape then she wouldn't be able to continue. Not that she wanted to, but what if she had a glass of wine later and decided to do one more, just to make certain no one would beat her? If she closed the programme she'd have to ~~start over. If she left it open, it wouldn't commit her to any~~thing. It simply gave her options. She always liked to give herself options. It was one of the things successful people did. She would do some more work then make a final decision as to whether to call that her highest score.

So she Alt-Tabbed to Facebook again and scrolled through new notifications. She didn't even know why she did that. The list of birthdays and drunken photos and local for-sales and baby photos and images of people doing yoga outdoors and recipes and ... Twitter was just as bad. Pictures of cats did nothing for her, and hashtags seemed so desperate.

Another realisation: if Facebook and Twitter disappeared tomorrow, she would let out a sigh of relief. When absence formed, something could fill it. But when things were already full, how could you fit anything new in? And without anything new, life became stale, and boring. And easy.

Alt-Tab.

DELETED: C:\Windows\Fonts\Comic Sans MS

No loss there.

DELETED: C:\Windows\Installer\10ee54a.msi

Digital crud.

DELETED: D:\music\E\(Everything But The Girl) Missing [Remix].mp3

Oh. She'd liked that song. But then again, she couldn't remember the last time she listened to it. Just one of thousands. No real loss.

Six files deleted. The screen now waited for a decision on "#7/20 - Random File".

This was so silly. She'd surely won by now. Olive Oil-Eyed Malcolm would never go any further. And yet, it wasn't as difficult as she'd expected. She'd imagined losing critical parts of her life. Maybe there was more padding around those parts than she'd realised. What the hell.

DELETED: C:\Windows\System32\es-ES\ comdlg32.dll.mui

No idea. Couldn't be important.

This wasn't a game. Not for the reason she'd originally thought – because it was more of a torture – but because all you had to do was click a button. Anyone could do it. Like this –

DELETED: D:\current\money\accounts\Bank\ flow5-4curr.xlsx

As soon as she saw that she pressed backspace but it did nothing. There *was* no Ctrl-Z option. Her personal finance spreadsheet was gone. It was last year's, but she still felt a flickering of ... excitement. The file had included a record of all her online purchases over a twelve-month period. All gone, just like that. A gap in her records. A neat, rectangular space.

She took a deep breath. She should get back to her proposal. She'd made her point.

And yet she was smiling. And she was nearly halfway there.

She'd been wrong when she said this wasn't a game. It *was* a game. Just not a game of skill. This was a test of courage and commitment. And she was more than equal to it.

DELETED: D:\current\odds\recipes\recipes_sweet.doc

She hadn't got round to trying half of those anyway. She didn't need them when she knew how to make failcake by heart.

The wording was different now. If she continued then the next time would be more than a file.

#10/20 - Random Folder

Her gut twisted. But it was impossible to separate the results of sickness from that of being at the top of a rollercoaster. Maybe they had always been the same thing.

A folder.

It could contain any number of files.

She could stop.

Why would someone make software like this?

She clicked.

DELETED: *D:\photos\older\2008\odds\Ludlow December*

Oh. A romantic holiday. They'd rented a cottage and gone there for New Year's Eve. Roaring log fire. Bottles of *frizzante*.

Sex in the afternoon. Artisan chocolates. For a second the heat returned, the fizz, the excitement ... and the loss.

But exes were exes. You couldn't go back. Wouldn't want to. Going backwards was always a mistake. Better to keep going forwards, keep looking for what you really wanted. The next .exe.

#11/20 - Random File

Ah, back to single files. They were easy.

Deleted: a photo.

Deleted: a file she had never heard of.

Deleted: a ... oh.

Oh.

DELETED: S:\central   filestore\management\ shared\training\services session\11-29 hea talk.pptx

Crap. That was a networked shared drive her laptop had mapped to. Trina hadn't realised that was still connected or accessible to software or ... or even who the file belonged to. It was in a shared folder of work in progress.

Gone.

Of course, there would probably be backups, and ... Her heart beat faster. It was just a talk but it could have been *anything* in her work folders. Software for the masochist in all of us.

The screen said "#14/20 - Random File".

Nothing had been a disaster.

She reached for her coffee, to quench the sudden dryness in her mouth, but the cup was empty.

What was she doing?

Winning. And it felt good as ever.

Deleted file #14 was a text file in a Program Files folder. The next was:

DELETED: D:\important\system   backups\Firefox\ bookmarks.html

The path gave her a start at first – it was the same folder branch that contained her list of passwords. A file that was itself password protected. But ... it hadn't been that file. It was just an export of her bookmarks. She hardly used them now anyway when everything was only one typed word away. One day she had looked at her bookmarks, with nested folders and lists that scrolled beyond the screen, and realised that she had been involved in a one-woman attempt to catalogue the Internet. Half the things were sites that she intended to look at later, and never did. In fact, when she'd set up the browser on this laptop, she hadn't bothered importing them. So they were gone for good.

Terror-relief-satisfaction. A surprisingly pleasant mix, with a newness like fresh plastic and canvas, neatly packaged as a pair in a box. A freshness that felt like cleanness.

#16/20 - Random File

No reason to stop now.

#16 was another .dll file, whatever they were. She clicked again.

DELETED: D:\historical\2011\2011_diary.doc

That was a year's worth of diary entries. She'd started keeping them as Word documents rather than paper books a year or so before that. She wasn't fastidious about filling it in, but usually made time after big events, or occasionally did a catchup summary within it. She didn't know why. Seeing that the file was gone for good ... it was another gap being created.

Another release.

It reminded her of the huge market for personal paper shredders. Normal people weren't shredding documents for security, despite what they claimed. They were doing something that fulfilled a deeper psychological need they didn't even recognise.

#18/20 - Random File

The past was irrelevant. The challenge is always in the now. She clicked delete.

DELETED: D:\photos\older\1988\Trina and Dad in snow (year a guess).jpg

She could picture that in her mind. A blurry photo because of the wind-whipped snowflakes obscuring much of the image, caught in a camera's flash that made the background black. And between the black and the white she stood, holding her dad's hand. One of the photos she'd scanned during an abortive process of digitally archiving things and throwing away the originals many years ago. Another memory that could never be refreshed by gazing on something real. It would fade.

She was rubbing her forearm again, and bit back anger that she wasn't in full control of this body, the one thing she should be, the one thing that was truly hers, the one thing … it was just for her and no one had a right, no one … She wiped her eyes with her palm. It was okay. She was in control. She was a winner. A 20/20 woman.

And she wasn't a fucking good girl.

Continue.

#19 was another work file from the shared drive. Costings from a tender related to a recent project. It was actually a disappointment after the photo had been wiped. She'd hoped for something to follow that would feel equally purging.

#20/20 - Random Folder

Only one to go and she'd be done. Going further and further than ever before, running through the pain and the lack of breath, refusing to give in. After coming this far, it was pointless to stop now. She clicked.

DELETED: C:\Windows\Help

And she'd done it. A list of twenty deletions. A short message congratulating her. Then only the option to play again or quit.

She rolled onto her back, hadn't realised how tense she'd been, tightly hunched over that small window. She imagined all the files disappearing. Then she looked around her room, and could picture the same in here, the virtual life somehow clearing out the real world too, pinging things out of existence, tidying up. Maybe with more space in her life she'd breathe easier. Maybe then she could start again, blank slate, fill life with something else. What, she didn't know yet. Places, options, people. It was just a feeling. But it existed. She was sure of it. It was clear. Win to end. And end to win.

Her list of deleted files was on the screen like a score. A crazy score only a psycho would have. A momentary honour, showing she had stood up to the world. Few people would have had the courage to do what she had done. She pressed Print Screen, the equivalent of her victory lap. She could print it on a T-shirt. Wear it to work. Let the men try and stare at her tits *then*.

She pasted the image into a document and saved it to the desktop.

In the end even this challenge was done. She rescanned the list of deleted files. It seemed pitiful compared to the fear she'd felt. And it hadn't deleted her new work proposal, the pending victory that would take her up to the next level.

And yet ... that work proposal didn't excite her like it had yesterday. It was running on the flat. Too easy. A place she'd reach in a few paces.

What was beyond it if she continued, running further and further than ever before, without stopping until she collapsed? What would be left of her then?

She rested her hand on the laptop lid, ready to close it. Of course, questions led to other questions.

Just idle curiosity, but how many files were there in total on a hard drive? And the work network?

Life was so easily turned into data and numbers that could then last forever, defining her past. Except that was also holding her in it. Stopping her from putting on a pair of new running shoes and heading in a different direction; not to anywhere known, but to *newness*. And she could imagine enjoying that run.

It was only 8.40 p.m., and she had the whole weekend.

She clicked Play Again.

Cry, Wolf

IT'S ALL RIGHT LADS, I'LL get this round in. Got to treat your mates, eh? Friends are the important ones in life. Hey, put it away, I said *I'll* pay, right? Good. What? No, no, it's fine. The stupid, silly bitch. You can't notice everything, no one can listen to all the shit you get off 'em. Jesus, they're all fuckin' neurotic. Yeah, drink to that! That's the ticket. Gasping, I was. And that heat! It's not so bad once the rooves are on, you got some shelter then. It's all right for you brickies, get shade from the scaffolding, don't you? My arse! You don't know what work is! Ah, true, that's the work, getting home. Huh, they say you should listen more, but so much is white noise, I'm no expert, I missed if it was ever there mixed in with the nonsense. Ha ha, quite a crowd, we own the pub tonight. Honest workers, not them woofters in suits. Yeah, cheers! Hey, check out him on darts. Thud thud, can't hit the board for toffee. The wall gonna be full of holes by the time he's finished. Hey, mate, you need new glasses! Yeah, you! Like bottle bottoms, limp-wristed fucker. Danger to others, that one. Always others. That time she left the gas on, fuck me I was furious, hundred 'n' one things I've got to watch out for without getting home and facing kingdom-fuck-come if I'd switched the light on. Scratchings, please. You? You? Okay, two packets. Best I'll get. I wish! Here's an example: sat at the dinner table. You should be happy, I sez, you love food! But no, just sat crying. Quiet, like, but running down over her fat cheeks. Even when I told her to knock it off. No one wants to see that, you make an effort, don't you? Hey, will you turn the juke box down, people are talking over here? Stuff them, it's not even music, just noise! Oh for fuck's sake. I swear, I'm gonna stop coming in here one day. They'll be fucking sorry when they stop seeing my notes. It's like they only want kids in nowadays. Nah, glad we never had sprogs. I hate them. All the crisp packets they leave outside my house, the noise they make – yeah, it's on the route to the junior one. But I get the last laugh. Check this, right. I always walk the dog near the school, let it shit on the bit of grass outside where the parents stand yacking while the kids run wild, right little bastards, and I leave the shit there, hope some of them will slip in it, get it on their faces or hands. Serve 'em right. Shit for shits. You get it? Shit for shits! Ha ha. Oh boy, who's dropped a glass. That's what they're cheering – oh what a fucking pillock. Shaky hand, what's he nervous about? Sure, same again. That's the thing, it's us that have it hard. Proper working, not in shops. It's an easy life for them. One, plenty of money; two, lots of free time; three, telly; four, house; five, can go hairdressers and stuff, do herself up. Only one thing to do, keep home. And keep her mouth shut around busybodies. You have to watch who they're knocking about with, no gossiping witches, no loose tongues, you have to come down heavy on them, like at the canals last year with the spotty pricks on bikes, kids thinkin' they're men. Fuck off, they won't get lippy again! Back in five, I'm bustin' for a leak.

NEEDED THAT. HEY, WHERE'S TOFFO gone? Home? What a lightweight. I always knew it about him. You can tell just by looking at some people. Put it away, my turn. Ha ha, see, he knows better than to argue about it with me! I still got it! Nah, not angry. You always got to keep a cool head. Rule number one. In the past I wasn't even angry when I had to get the message across, y'know? I know I can lose it sometimes, but I hardly laid a fucking finger, not even a gut punch or – you know, not even a fucking arse slap. Hands off, nothin' to write home about. What? You believe that? All that shit, "time of the month", FUCK OFF YOU'RE LAUGHING AT ME I said, only a bit of a tap, just some sense, that should have been nowt but it was maybe connected, and who knows what goes on in their heads, eh? Bleeding hearts. You married? Exactly. So you know shit diddly about it. Yeah, fuck off, we didn't want you coming with us anyway! Only 'cos we felt sorry for you, you gormless fucking Scouser! Ha ha, see him scuttle off? I know, I know, not like the old crew. Real workers. Half of 'em now hardly speak English, not proper anyway. What if they're helping a sparky and put the wrong wire in? Ha ha, zappo! But it's serious. Someone could end up ... Oh, I know it. When they rang me, said she was in hospital,

I bottled it up, the fury, last thing I wanted was some long-nosed busy twat sticking it in. But fuck, natural to be angry, amiright? What she did attracted attention. I was nice in hospital, and you know what, I laughed – the dozy cow had cut across the wrists, not even through the tendons, that does fuck all, something she'd seen on telly I bet, or read in Mills and Boon; if she'd sliced up the forearm, into the artery, there'd have been no muckin' about. It was just for show. Attention. That's the last fucking thing I needed. What? Pool? Games are for the kids, I'm not having any of that. What's up with talking? Oh, right, seen your arse, eh? Yeah, you go and clack your balls together, us three will stay and talk proper. Fucking pool, eh? Blowing money. Need owt from the bar, lads? Oh no, you can't go too! I know it's not my round, but I insist, just stay a bit more. I'll get them. Stay right the fuck there.

HERE WE GO. CHEERS, EARS. What? Course! How can you not like your wife? Or be used to them, anyway, which is the same thing. No one wants change. Marriage is somethin' you have to work at. Both of you. Sure, out of the hospital. But I already lined up in my head that she needed talkin' to. Rule number one. Course, I tried to be nice about it. "First and last time," I told her back home, "you dozy fat cunt, stop snivelling, do a proper job or do fuck all," and I meant it so she *wouldn't*, you know? To get her straight. And she was so upset I went easy on her even though that blubbering face just made me angry. What's the point in snivellin'? People walk all over you. Got to be best foot forward.

"What if the fucking neighbours hear about it, do you want that, ashamed of the crying blob of the street? Always thinking of your fucking lazy-arsed self!" Believe me, you don't want to get my attention this way. So I went easy on her. Maybe I knocked her about a bit, but I think under the circumstances ... Anyway, that was it. Things back to normal. Happy enough. Aw no, you don't really ... right. Just fucking go. Like the rest of 'em, you are. Never mind, Mick, just you and me, old son. Don't need the others. You're right, better out than in. Like puking, right? Course it hurts. How do you think I feel, eh, she lets me down like this? I knew she had pills but those doctors are to blame, shouldn't't've given her so many when there's nowt wrong with her in the first place a little talking to couldn't sort out. They did this! And now she's stress-free, laughing at me I bet ... I swear it looked like she was smiling even with the puke on her chin, gob full of it, dirty cow, and I ... I never thought she'd do it proper ... How the fuck was I supposed to know? And – shit – she was worthless – useless – and now – now she's not here ... Nah, I'm fine. Hey, you don't really need to be getting back. It's early! Just one more drink, a snack. I'm out, look, spent up. Will you get me one? Aw, go on! So what if she's waiting? She's losing her hair! What you looking at me like that for? What's love got to ... Oh, fuck off then with you, piss off back to her. I don't need you, or any of youse. Waste of fucking space. Everyone's so prickly nowadays. Got to be practically correct or whatever. Fuck it. Hey! Yes, you, if you could stop chatting and start serving like you're paid for ... Can I have one and put it on my tab? I'm always in here! I don't know your face either, love. Check with Tom. He'll vouch. Well ring him then! I don't like your attitude either, you stuck-up cow. You're meant to be serving ... call them then, I know the bouncers here. Yo, you're Paddy, right? She was – hey, get your hands off me. Just listen, I only want a drink! Don't make me go, okay, I'll behave. Why you all looking at me? How'd you like it if you had to go home and ... and the house is so empty now. Now the fa– ... now she ain't there. I ... no, let me go, I'm just sniffing, you fucking dick, you don't know what it's like! None of youse do! I hate going to bed! Goose pimples all down my arms, stupid cunt, aren't I, soft, but – it's so empty. Fuckin' hell, how were I supposed to know? How ... why didn't she ... it's not my ... oh God ... Oh God.

The Potential

ONCE UPON A TIME A man lived on his own in a castle.

Not really on his own, since he had a ferocious dog called Tara. A beast with long teeth and shining eyes and a wet tongue that could lick fiercely.

Not really a ferocious dog then, but she did bark at people who walked down the passage beyond the back garden, prompting angry shouts and thrown items which made her bark all the more.

Not really a castle then, more of a terraced house on an old road that had been partly encircled by a cheaply built new estate of identical small tower blocks. Now they *did* resemble castles, with the river beyond as a kind of moat and rusting balconies that faced in every direction and could be used to pour boiling oil on attackers. If not boiling oil, then at least bottles and piss.

It flooded from time to time, which the council knew when it granted planning permission, but thanks to a special friendship between some of the councillors and the developers, that report was left at the bottom of the pile and by the time of the first flooding it was too late to do anything about it except write letters to the local paper. The councillors responsible had moved on and the griping fell to a low grumble that only rose with the water levels.

The man's back garden was narrow and short. He wished it was long like the grass, part of the tangled confusion of plants that Tara loved to sniff around. In the lush chaos of undergrowth and trees lived slugs and snails which slid up and down his house at night leaving shining trails for the morning sun; snails which fed the thrushes, slugs which fed the hedgehogs (and, once, Tara, but she spat most of the sticky mollusc back out unchewed).

The man did not like other people. He felt like he'd always had a rum deal. An outsider. Slower, uglier, different, in-the-way. The first to go when they had to "make savings". He'd become a self-employed electrician eventually, so no one could dump him, and he only had to deal with one person at a time. In, out: potentials measured, fuses replaced and faces forgotten.

Tara and his garden had been the exception, the one place he was accepted as himself. The slugs and snails were fine company, and easy. Sometimes he went out at night with his torch and watched them eating windfall apple, or bread he'd left out for the hedgehogs, mouths chewing away slowly, eyes at the end of stalks gently surveying. Tara would lie at his side and occasionally lick his hand. At those peaceful times he was as happy as he'd known.

These gardens were abundant emeralds amid the encroaching grey of the urban areas. As well as the estate on what was once a meadow floodplain, the local fields he'd pl... become a school and a care home; the woods h[a]s a lad had skate park and car park. It was strange how parks ... out for a be green. When they'd been built the council had s... er had to in tune with the surroundings, and that was kind of ... 'y'd be remaining straggling trees were hardly noticeable, an... the ...ere outnumbered by the new streetlights alongside the new ceme... d paths above the new channels dug for power cables that sever... the roots of a third of the remaining trees. The council ecologist hadn't objected, saying in her report that she'd detected no wildlife there of meritable conservation status (in the afternoon when she'd spent five minutes in the woods before having lunch in her car and texting the local businessman she was having an affair with).

In many people's eyes the changes were good because they made things tidier and easier to maintain. You don't have to trim hedges if you get rid of the hedges, and don't need to sweep up leaves if there are no trees. Though, strangely, as the trees and hedges disappeared, more litter blew around the paths. Town administrators just shrugged. Understanding such mysteries was beyond the ken of any of the land's wise men.

Such is the way of things, and the old man knew it. Oh, he knew it. Because he *was* old. Once tall and strong, he was now gangly and wispy-haired with ears that seemed too large for his head and shirts that hung too large on his body. Kids pointed and laughed at him when he limped to the local shops. They called him The Elephant Man.

meadow floodplain, the local fields he'd played in as a lad had become a school and a care home; the woods hollowed out for a skate park and car park. It was strange how parks no longer had to be green. When they'd been built the council had said they'd be in tune with the surroundings, and that was kind of true – the remaining straggling trees were hardly noticeable, and were outnumbered by the new streetlights alongside the new cemented paths above the new channels dug for power cables that severed the roots of a third of the remaining trees. The council ecologist hadn't objected, saying in her report that she'd detected no wildlife there of meritable conservation status (in the afternoon when she'd spent five minutes in the woods before having lunch in her car and texting the local businessman she was having an affair with).

In many people's eyes the changes were good because they made things tidier and easier to maintain. You don't have to trim hedges if you get rid of the hedges, and don't need to sweep up leaves if there are no trees. Though, strangely, as the trees and hedges disappeared, more litter blew around the paths. Town administrators just shrugged. Understanding such mysteries was beyond the ken of any of the land's wise men.

Such is the way of things, and the old man knew it. Oh, he knew it. Because he *was* old. Once tall and strong, he was now gangly and wispy-haired with ears that seemed too large for his head and shirts that hung too large on his body. Kids pointed and laughed at him when he limped to the local shops. They called him The Elephant Man.

A public footpath bordered the end of his garden. It ran from the tower blocks to the main road, so was always busy. There used to be a low fence separating his garden from the path, but he got tired of everyone staring in, eyes destroying privacy as he pottered around. So he used most of his savings for a higher fence. That brought its own problems. Kids rattled his gate as they walked past. They threw things over the barrier, crisp packets and bags of dog poo, and worse, meaning he had to collect litter most days, so Tara didn't cut her paw on a can or bottle. They taunted him over the fence and ran away if he approached it. At night-time they'd sometimes dare each other to climb the fence and throw stones or eggs at his house, making him shudder at the impacts, knowing they invaded his space with impunity. Shouts would wake him in the night. One time he used the normally bolted gate to get on to the footpath himself, and he saw that the other side of his fence had become a graffiti billboard for local expression. Balloon-like names, vulgar pictures and insults built up layer by layer, engulfing previous generations of paint. So many layers, from so many people.

Maybe they were jealous because he had his own garden.

The police said they would "talk to people" but could do nothing else without a name, a face, a description.

Other worries jumbled in his mind. The paper had been full of comments saying the town needed a Tesco and an M&S, because there was nowhere to shop nearby. He didn't understand it. There had always been shops at the end of the road. What would the supermarkets sell that was so much better? A tin of soup was a tin of soup wherever you bought it. Fewer local shops now, though, he admitted. Most people preferred to drive to the out-of-town industrial park. The greengrocer had shut last year, and the butcher and post office the year before. That only left the launderette and the hairdressers and the takeaway.

He had trees in the garden. They provided shelter from the sounds. But one day the council said they were unsafe, blocked neighbour's light, and the roots of the hundred-year-old oak were damaging the public footpath. The oak was completely removed and the other trees cut down to leafless stubs that the birds avoided. Then they sent him a bill. The green was gone, the nests were gone, replaced with stumps and bare emptiness. He knew the remains of the apple tree would not fruit next year. It would be in shock. As he was.

When he sat on his bench he had to face the other way now, it was too upsetting, and when he looked out of his back windows he didn't see tree tops, he saw the towers of the estate by day, their thousands of electric lights by night. It was as if they were in his garden now. He stopped looking out of those windows.

The birds didn't come back.

The oldest trees had been there before the estate, before the footpath. No one respected age any more. Age was a bad thing to be cleared away and carted off on the back of a truck. And he was a stone, ground down by ages, bone powder scraping away at his joints.

Tara was old too. Not as fast as she used to be, and grey around the muzzle. Mostly obedient, but you can't teach old dogs new tricks, and she had one bad habit – barking at anyone on the path if she heard voices. Maybe she still thought it was her territory. The garden had been longer once, but the council had done a compulsory purchase for the estate's new footpath. When he'd fought it, the letters in the local paper filled with venom, directed at him: he was a selfish old man. He lost. The garden was shortened.

Tara barked even more after the trees were cut. Voices and laughter and shouting from the passage seemed louder, echoey, no longer a muffled sound blocked by leaves. It aggravated the old dog, and the more she barked the more it became a kids' game to taunt her, and an adults' game to shout at her, and to tell the old man to shut his motherfucking crazy cunt of a dog up. He tried to quiet her but she picked up on his tension when anyone walked down the passage, and she barked even more. The police came one time and told him he was disturbing the peace. He tried to explain but the unspoken accusation "selfish" was in his mind. Their hints at "dog control byelaws" made him think of Tara being taken away like the trees and that was the final straw, so he didn't let Tara out in the garden on her own any more. She would lie by the back door, whining, and he had to say no, and try to distract her, but old dogs and old habits stay and it hurt her, and it hurt him.

And once upon this magic time she was barking as the older kids jeered, but then she yelped, and the voices faded as the kids ran off while the old man moved over as quickly as he could and he found her lying on her side breathing fast, her eye a mess of blood from the broken brick they'd thrown over, and he held her and tried to stop her using her dew claw to scratch the cracked brow while she whimpered.

The vet did what he could but the bone there had shattered. She lost the eye. When bone breaks, character does too. She didn't bark much after that, just whined in the night. It was difficult to get her to go in the garden, she would just cower near the house, and she took to pissing on the kitchen floor, even though she'd always been such a clean dog before. He didn't scold her. He just mopped it up while she lay, head on paws, making a strange high-pitched wheeze. Could dogs feel shame? He thought so. It stung to see her life and happiness so drained. Stolen.

More changes were coming. Ancient tales always require a dragon or a pestilence or a witch's curse. Plans move ahead, announced only when it was too late to stop them because the momentum was great enough to carry forward over all obstacles. The houses on his road had been sold, each neighbour giving in, taking what was offered rather than lose in the long run. One by one they took the money and left, and their homes became empty shells waiting for the inevitable. But the old man refused. This was his *home*. He didn't know anywhere else. The suggestions that he'd be better off getting rid of his dog and moving into the old people's home terrified him. Once people went in there you never saw them again, except as blank, pale faces at windows. He was told he couldn't remain: compulsory purchase would be enacted if he was stubborn. He fought with letters but they ignored him, said it was imperative for the vitality of the town, he was blocking development. The council hired a swish law firm that represented the big supermarkets, they all threatened to take him to court, amazing what you could afford with public money. He couldn't see any way to win against that.

189

He had nightmares of bulldozers and impatient councillors and roads, all encroaching, taking, turning the green to grey. And the gardens would make way for a car park and a new construction that reached for the sky as a temple to call all around. A temple of choice. But no, they would not wait. It had to be now, according to demographics and market demand. He was being selfish in trying to stop progress. And the council had already paid the supermarkets an enticement to come here, to bring their bounty. This was an investment. Investments can't be halted for the individual.

He continued to write letters by hand in spidery writing, but they seemed weak and flimsy compared to the solid blocks of text and thick paper he received in return.

Tara died in the night a few months later. He found her stiff body in the morning. It took him hours to dig her grave but he did it, alone, as deep a pit as he could manage near where the oak tree had been, and planted flower seeds on top from an old packet. They were probably long past germination, but maybe a trace of nature's magic could break through. His back ached when he stood and returned to the quiet house.

He lost his appetite, such as it had been. Took to going out less, too. Tried to block out the world by turning up the volume on his TV. No dog by his side to stroke and calm his hands. They shook when he didn't pay attention to them. He was going to lose his home.

He understood the problem well enough, but he couldn't put it in words. The land division system seemed to be broken. Apparently councils cut the land up into blocks on a map, marked as residential, commerce, agriculture, or whatever "development" categories they felt like in conjunction with those who had the influence and money to suggest it. Objections from anyone else got nowhere. It was a biased system that led to blocks of only one type of thing, all across the land. Fields would have houses crammed on since the whole thing was marked as "residential", rather than saying it was to be half housing, half native forest. And the categories were inherently unfair. The councils didn't mark large blocks of land for re-wilding, or nature conservation, or tree-planting. They only chose categories that generated money.

Then one day he stood by Tara's grave as cold November bit, his breath a mist and fingers numb, cheeks stinging, trying to remember the peace of green summers past. The memories couldn't come, though, buried in earth too hard to let anything out.

The reverie broke when he heard a laugh: seemingly the same laugh he'd heard so many times before, part of a crowd of juvenile voices chanting "Where's your dog-gie gone? *Where'syourdoggiegone?*" to some tune he half recognised. This was too much, and something snapped inside, and he hobbled to the gate at the bottom of the garden, threw it open to watch the kids scarper, but he spotted the one he hated most, in his bright jacket and shaved head, a look of amusement turning to surprise as he saw the old man; although the others ran off this boy stuck two fingers up and stayed, not expecting the old man to approach, not expecting him to grab the orange padded hood of his coat and start yanking it around, tears in the old man's eyes as he shouted that the boy was a disgrace, had no respect, and the boy twisted and kicked out and in turn told him to fucking get off, yelling that he was a paedo, the boy getting red in the face at this unexpected turn, teary with anger and frustration that he couldn't break free from the grip, his hood stretching and beginning to tear while his threats of what his brothers would do to the man went ignored.

Some of the other boys came back now, jeering and pointing at both of them, getting bolder and moving in.

In every fairy story there's a fork in the road. The side that runs straight and narrow to town, and the road that leads off into the shadowy woods.

The winding wooded path, then. This boy was a ringleader. This boy's nasal voice always seemed to be there, calling obscenities over the fence. This boy stood for all of them. The estate people, the council, the police, the doctors ... and the boy's head connected with the wall, half-accident at first but enough to silence everyone, so the old man shoved it again, thud, thud, the boy at a bad angle to resist, and finally having a look of fear on that bloodied face, fear that would have to do in place of respect, smack smack as the others ran in to try and separate them, too late, the old man smashed that head against the brick wall again and again before they pulled him off, wanting to break all that bone on good solid brick, show them what it was like when faces mushed to pulp ... a sacrifice was always one for the many, and a sacrifice was always red. The wall was smeared in blood, bright spatters of sickening crimson on the floor around the broken teenager.

He spent his last few years in prison, treeless concrete and steel. He lay on the bed of guilt and hate in his cell and knew they were vandalising his garden, smashing house windows, celebrating their expulsion of the limping bogeyman in communal togetherness, and he knew he'd die without ever seeing that garden again, the building would go ahead, the supermarkets, the car park, and Tara would be buried under concrete just as he was, alone and forgotten.

So much for the wooded shadow path. It flashed up in a second after the first time that face scraped against the wall, and the redness of the blood brought back Tara's pain ... the pain was too much. The shadow path was not for him, any more than the man-made highway. So he took another. He stopped at the fork, let them pull the boy away, swearing and crying at the old man, but the boy's face was only scratched, not broken. The old man lowered himself to the ground with a sigh, tried to ignore the group anger around him, and waited for the police to arrive.

He was in trouble. Not the prison of broken faces, but instead – equally to the glee of developers and supermarkets and planning departments – declared unsafe to live alone. So he was moved to the old people's home nearby, his house finally purchased for a nominal fee, the money used to pay for his care ... and so returning to the council coffers week by week.

The old man's face joined the other slack visages watching as the bulldozers and diggers and demolition vehicles moved in. It was surprisingly quick for all that history to be turned to rubble and carted away, the ground dug over, plants removed, foundations laid. As the speckled, flat surface was laid bare, so was the truth in the old man's eyes: construction is destruction.

Up rose the skeletal steel structures that would house the new body, amid days of grinding and machinery and clanging and dust. Much of the work was hidden behind the billboards that lined the site, showing images of happy consumers gazing up at the completed shopping centre with the eyes of the devout, watercolour trees bordering the images in a fit of dishonesty (or imagination, as they called it in the trade). Hardly any graffiti graced those billboards; on the few occasions when a tag appeared, the council quickly cleaned it off. During the spring the electrics and plumbing and walls and floors were prepared, and the old man watched, and muttered to himself, and wished, and something stirred inside his heart. Something strange and vital, a concoction that took its flavour from whatever was added, past and present; that would grow whether hate was poured into it, or love. It could only be one or the other. That's how spells work, and the caster makes the choice.

And he sat, and watched, and fed the thing inside. And when it was so big it felt like it would explode from his chest, he went to bed.

In some ways the story ended here.

But let's go just a bit further. After all, magic always happens just beyond the normal boundaries.

It is a Sunday morning in mid-April.

The building site is quiet, too early for the weekend workers yet.

A mist hangs heavy in the air, clinging to the ground like a lover to their desire, knowing morning light means the night's end approaches. It begins to dissipate as the world wakes, movement swirling the air currents and the sun burning away at hanging vapours. As it fades it reveals a changed landscape.

The first person is a morning runner, who jogs past the site while worrying about her throbbing shin splints, then retraces her steps to stare.

A dog walker joins her. The dog disappears into the new terrain, barking happily, and their human doesn't notice, they are so busy gawping.

A newspaper delivery boy on his bike skids to a halt.

The first of the builders arrives. Instead of just staring, he heads over to the roots, examines them, looking for tell-tale signs of a digger. But if there were any signs, the moss and foliage hides them.

Groups attract others, growing the mass, increasing its gravity, until there are many groups staring and talking. Some whisper reverently, some jabber excitedly, many take photos and videos on their phones.

There'd been a vast area of concrete and steel the night before, with construction machinery and piles of beams and spools of cable and pallets of tiles and bags of plaster and cement. They are all gone. Poof!

In their place is a forest. A mature, native forest of old oak trees and yew and silver beech and ash, supporting wild undergrowth and a whole carpet of bluebells. The noise of drilling and shouting has been replaced with birdsong, and moving machinery replaced with the stirring of leaves in a refreshing morning breeze.

More people arrive. Some explore the woods and come out wide-eyed in astonishment, carrying some of the peace out with them, smiling at the gathering crowds. Reporters turn up. People are interviewed. Film crews aren't far behind. A helicopter flies over, filming the site from above, the unbroken green canopy which has replaced the nascent Tesco/M&S combo. They share it on TV, alongside an image of how the site had looked a few days earlier. Many of those watching the news think it is a joke, and check to see if it is April 1st again.

The council staff arrive, along with the contracted developers. For once they don't seem so smug. A huddled discussion follows, citing costs and delays, and orders are given to cut down the trees. The first construction worker refuses. Something shines in his eyes as he looks at the forest. Recognition, maybe. The second refuses as well. The third builder is offered a huge bonus, but as he climbs into the digger, thinking it might be easiest to break down some of the smaller trees and dig up the brush, there is such an uproar from the crowd that he switches off the engine and jumps down. "Not worth it," he mutters.

The council works with the police. Cordons are set up. People are told to keep out of the beautiful woodland "for their own safety". After all, isn't it still technically a construction site? There are scuffles. Shouts that it is public land, that people have rights. More police arrive, more angry meetings held. Professional tree fellers are brought in. On seeing the forest some of them refuse too. Others agree to have a go. They couldn't make much impact but they are told it will be symbolic. Do their best. The pay would be huge. Despite the booing and yelling from the growing crowd they succeed in taking down one of the trees after removing as many upper branches as they can first. It creaks slowly, as if moaning, resisting, but finally falls with an almighty crash, sending up clouds of leaves. The birds go quiet and the crowd is silenced.

Then the fighting begins. People who'd done nothing as shreds were stripped from green spaces, slivers peeled back here and there, criss-crossed with paths and roads like scars: suddenly they are incensed.

Many are wounded. Many break through and wander the forest in amazement. Prayers are made. A camp is set up at the edge of the site. People share food and drinks and stories and music, and bring their children, and always there is this reverence.

News of the situation goes global. It may have only happened in this one small place, a tiny, localised miracle in the grand scheme of things, but the feeling it touches in hearts spreads. If there's love and magic then there's also hope, and that's often what people need. Advertising tries to sell it, but it's always empty, dissipates like mist. For once this was the real thing, substantial as day. And the dream was free to all. The council would have a hard time pushing through their Regeneration Masterplan now, a plan that had cost the taxpayer £163,000 from a consultancy firm in London.

The scientists couldn't explain it (but had fun trying). Other people said it didn't need explaining. One woman, who looked like she'd been crying, told the camera crew, "The potential was there all along." No one really knew what that meant but it made a nice headline, so various news outlets used it as their lead.

One of the smaller magazines, which went mostly unread, had a different take on the event: they pointed out that regardless of what amazing thing had happened here, it didn't actually require a miracle to achieve it. People had the power to preserve or create the same anywhere. If we wanted miracles then we could have them in every backyard, every street. We just had to want them enough.

The news did not report on the old man who'd died in the care home facing the new forest, taking his last breaths the same night as the miracle happened. Why should they? He was just another old man dying in the background while bigger things happened, with no family left to write even the blandest obituary. But sometimes it takes one for the many. It's the trick, not the magician, and that story ended as another began. As to whether people lived happily ever after ... that's for someone else to tell.

Miasma

HE KEPT HIS SARNIES IN his pocket, no appetite for food yet, stomach flip-flopping with excitement, dark hair pulled from his eyes, Dad's thick gardening gloves slipped on, sleeves tucked in, scratchproof. He checked to make sure no one else was in this thin bit of woods by the stream, especially adults, but it was just him and creaking branches overhead as vast green treetops caught enough wind to bend stiff limbs; he hunched, careful in opening the box, dark crack inside, not big enough for escape – that had happened once before – then quick grab in, hold of fur, head, and now the cat squealed as he pulled it out; he licked sweat from his lips whilst getting a firm grip on the hissing, spitting creature, so much stronger than its size. He couldn't hold it up for long, so knelt by the water's edge and thrust it under, gripping with fingers pinched tight into muscle and folded skin while it struggled, bubbled, splashed ferociously with panic, he muttered "Just a test" but held it under, waiting for it to weaken before ipulling it out; pushing it through terror to resignation, then

pulling it out; pushing it through terror to resignation, then offering the wet rag hope, heavier in his arms sympathetically tired, before he dropped it coughing and crawling in mud, pulling towards life. It passed the test, and as he started to stab it with a pocket knife it bled into that mud, rich red, too tired to mewl loud, its voice not reaching the road beyond the wood, the road to the farm where the bull lay in bellows of pain, refusing to stand as it was kicked. "Its leg's broke," one man said, pointing. "Went through the grate, slipped." "We haven't got time for this," snapped the other, fetching the prod from the cabin. "Get up you lazy bastard!" It bellowed in ear-shattering vibration as he prodded it in the testicles again and again, cursing and kicking the useless animal. Further up, two miles away in the factory, blood and stinking parts unsuitable for rendering were sprayed down the gulley, high-pressure water merging with the dark-stained juices below chains as it blasted the floors from brown to red to pink to almost white before the next batch of lowing, panicked animals were dragged in. That blood and water filtered from the abattoir along artificial veins in the earth, dead, seeking rejuvenation in a heart that doesn't exist, filtering into mud stained brown, Earth's kidneys, washed out in streams and into the reservoir above, all town water filtered from there, micro-polluted with the essence of suffering, labelled "pure", into pipes, tanks, the tap he poured his glass of water from. He drank it then returned to the counter, woman with a boy, cute boy, dark hair in his eyes. "What you want?" the man asked, solid arms planted square. "Half a pound of ham for his sarnies." She rubbed the boy's scruffy hair. He flinched away uncomfortably, readjusting that dark fringe to hide his eyes and watching the cold precision of circular saw slicing thin cuts on to crisp paper, limp and dead and no longer struggling.

14

"STUFF ON THE STORMS? WINDS of ninety miles an hour. Floods in –"

"Nah. Jost city people whingin' an whinin' like women." His dad waved the fly swatter irritably. "Won't affect us, touch wood," he added, patting the leg of his chair.

Robbie turned the crinkling page. "One here on Prince Charles and his kids. Sez they did a conference ... to save rhinos and stop hunting and stuff ... but turns ite Harry and Will went hunting in Spain, shot loads of wildlife."

"Fer pity's seek. Don't wanna know abite them spoilt bastards."

Next was an article on illegal immigrants. Robbie skipped it and turned another crinkling page. No point setting his dad off.

"Theer's one on ducks here."

"Ducks?"

"Flappy ones. Ruddy ducks, it sez. Being killed. The Government and the RSPB want to wipe 'em ite."

"Go on."

He read from The Daily Mail article, detailing the cull. "Then it sez 'More than five and a half thousand killed so far, and only arind twenty are left in the UK'. Wow. Only twenty."

"I've heard of that. In winter we used to get loads. Mostly wiped ite now. Daft birds – when they's breeding they hang arind, even if yer shooting at 'em. Too stupid to fly off."

"Maybe they see it as their land?"

"Not, is it, though? Belongs to us. People."

Robbie read on. "It sez this 'takes the total cost of the cull to nearly four million pounds.'"

"Four million? Fer fuck's seek. All that money but they want to shut the hospital ward? And meals on wheels fer the old uns?"

"The library mate be shut too," Robbie added. "Mrs Cooper told us. We'll have to go to the central one." Mrs Cooper. The best teacher he knew. She never made him feel like shrinking to nowt when he got questions wrong. She smelt good when she leaned over you. Clean. And she'd taught him the word *hypocrisy*. He thought of it now. *Four million pounds.*

"They'll come back anyways, the ones from Europe," said his dad. "Birds're like all the rest, always wanting to come over here. But if the London wankers want to spend so much on killing ducks that fuck too much, we can't stop 'em. Vermin on the ponds, vermin wi' the brass. Bad uns always win."

Robbie stared at a photo of a duck and picked out the details, his face close enough to inhale the inky smell of the finger-smudged newspaper.

"Hey, Dad. I think I've seen some of those. Pond at Potter's Fields."

"Which one?"

"Upbank from Bradnop's Brook."

"Near Green Edge weer the coloureds live?"

Robbie nodded.

"Whut you doing up theer?"

Robbie looked down, caught out. "I like it." His dad stared at him, uncomprehending eyes shaded by thick brows. He wanted more. "All sorts of plants growing up now cows aren't grazin' theer any more. Din't know theer'd be so much."

"Plants?" Dad shook his head. "Land's jost going to waste now Potter's dead," he grumbled.

Robbie scanned ahead to see if ... wow.

Now there is a £2,500 bounty on each coppery head, and one day the final ruddy duck will peer above the rushes and stare down the barrel of a hunting rifle.

He read it in silence again and gawped at the figure, thinking of all you could buy with £2,500. Like being a king, nothin' you couldn't do, and –

A loud thwack shattered the vision.

"Got the bastard!" his dad shouted triumphantly, wiping the fly swatter's gooey mess on the base of his chair. "Why'd you stop reading?"

"Were jost looking at other pieces. That's pretty much the end of it." He folded the newspaper over. "Am done wi' readin'."

"Rate." His dad sighed. "I suppose I'd best drive up to Bottomcote."

"Why?"

"The clippers are bost. Jost keeps snapping the suckers' teeth. I'll buy wirecutters in town, that'll do till I can get some proper clippers. Stop off at the pig sheds on way back. Fappy should be theer cleanin' the sows ite, fill the slurry tanks."

"John said one has a brock leg."

"Probably have to shoot it. I'll look in when am theer."

"Fappy kicks 'em."

"Jost to get 'em moving."

"Hits 'em too. With a bar."

"Aye? Better not be him that did its leg. He'll have to pay me. But fost things fost. Yer fourteenth. Whut dost want? Am not promising, mind."

"A phone," Robbie said, without hesitation.

"We've got one."

"A *mobile*. Everyone else at school has them."

Dad scratched at his rubbery nose. "I think I mate be able to do something. Fappy were getting rid of his."

Sudden panic. "No! A good one, one of them smart uns, not jost fer making phone calls."

"A phone that's not jost fer calls? Yer a button short! How much is that?"

"You can get 'em fer fifty pind."

"Fifty pind? Fer pity's seek. Think of something else. Whut abite trainers?"

Right. Robbie knew what they sold in the cheap shoe shop, next to the pub and the bookies. And his dad did too.

"I'll think abite it."

"You do. Want a lift to town?"

Robbie shook his head. Saturday. Most of the kids from school would be there.

Dad got up, held his hand out. "Gizzit." Robbie passed him the newspaper. "I wish you'd do something, not jost hang abite in the house, useless lump."

"Whut like?"

"Stop lookin' at fuckin' plants and make yerself useful. Get rid of some of the mess rind this place."

ROBBIE SAT AT THE KITCHEN table amid a sprawl of worn cloths, tools, and the mingled smells of cleaning solvents and lubricating oils.

He heard a noise outside. Getting nearer. Angry barking in the yard. He moved a brush up and down the metal tube to loosen any bits.

Mrs Broughton shuffled in, dragging the wheezing Benji by his lead and slamming the door behind her. The barking continued outside. Benji huffed. Such a wrinkle-faced unhealthy beast. He would never outrun Robbie's mongrel, Sabre. That's why Mrs Broughton had to bring Benji inside when she was doing for them, so Sabre wouldn't eat him. When Benji realised he was now safe from Robbie's dog he stopped cowering and waddled cockily off, sniffing the air.

E's a pure breed bulldog, sired by champions, she'd told him once.

E's a squashed-faced sad-looking thing wi' droopy eyes and jowls, Robbie had replied.

If you can't see the wolf, it's not a healthy dog.

"Ah do, duck," said Mrs Broughton.

He nodded.

She put the kettle on so she could wash the dishes piled up in the sink, then filled a water bowl for her slobbering dog. The plumbing continued to judder even after the tap was turned off.

Robbie dripped solvents on to the small mop attached to a twelve-inch rod. Gave them a quick sniff after checking she wasn't looking. He loved that nostril-flaring chemical smell. He ran the mop back and forth down each shotgun barrel.

"You should keep yer dog chained up," she said.

"E's alrate. Guards the place."

"From whut?"

"Burglars. Busybodies. Zombies."

"Yer talkin' a packer daft."

She started sorting out the dirty dishes. A farty squeeze of washing-up liquid into the stainless-steel sink. Cold water hissing in with a metal drum echo.

He rubbed away at traces of dirt and corrosion, burnishing the metal to a dull shine.

"Always in yer head. Not rate," she mumbled.

"It is rate."

He peered down each breech as he held it up to the window, seeing bright sky beyond the hard metal circles. All clear. He added a thin film of oil to the moving parts, checked they were free running, then ran the traces of oil up and down the outside of the barrel with a cloth. His dad didn't bother with that, which is why it showed traces of rust. Robbie looked after it better. He closed and latched the mechanism.

"You gonna be makin' something fer tea?" he asked.

"Yes. A pan of lobby."

Urgh. She always made lobby. And somehow ruined it. He could just picture the overcooked vegetables dissolving into the meaty mush.

"Great," he muttered.

"Worse weer theer's none, you ingrate. That's the thing wi' you, yer always thinking of yerself." She took the kettle and poured boiling water into the sink before scrubbing the cups and pans with her back to him. "Anyway, normal lads yer age would be ite wi' a girl on a Saturday. Not messing up the table."

"I ain't got a girl."

"No surprise, the state of you. If you took care of yerself a bit more you'd have one. Whut abite my Leanne?"

Mrs Broughton's granddaughter. Skinny, pale, big teeth: used to charge lads for a feel. "Not my type."

He lifted the gun, looked down the sights; rotated his upper body whilst holding it steady. The back of her head moved into the target.

"Beggars can't be choosers," said Mrs Broughton, arms deep in lather.

Robbie pulled back the hammer and latch. A click. It was ready to fire. Dishes clinked together in the sink. He moved his finger slowly from the trigger guard to the trigger itself.

Maybe she'd wondered at his silence: she turned, cloth in hand, and saw the gun barrel. Her eyes widened and she dropped a pan into the water, a gloopy splash sending suds over the edge of the sink to slop on the floor. Benji panicked and ran off.

"Whut!" she shrieked.

He lowered the gun. "It's okay. It's not loaded."

She held the washing cloth over her heart, making a wet patch on her tits. "You should never point a gun at someone!"

"It's nothin'."

"I'll tell yer dad! He'll belt yer!"

"Not fer this."

"You shouldn't even have it."

"He lets me. An' he needs it later. Am cleanin' it fer him."

He slid it into the padded shotgun bag. Took a handful of steel shot cartridges from the box, zipped them into the side pouch, a jumble of red plastic and brass-coloured caps. Death fireworks.

"Still –"

"Am goin' ite," he interrupted. "I'll tidy this up later. Jost leave it." He slipped the gun bag over his shoulder and left before she could have a go at him about anything else.

Sabre came bounding up to him in the yard and Robbie was tempted to leave the kitchen door ajar, let Sabre in for a Benji snack ... but no. Sabre would get in trouble.

"Come wi' me boy. You can walk me s'far as the lanes."

The dog trotted beside him. Then Robbie realised that he hadn't been paying attention. His foot was over a dark crack in the cement, which stretched out from the old drain. A deep fissure right under his feet, nearly two inches wide where he stood. He didn't like to imagine what crawled and squirmed down there.

He turned around three times, holding his breath, then spat on the ground. Sabre thought it was a game and started barking. But Robbie was now safe. He reached down and scratched Sabre behind the ears before they moved off at a brisk pace.

A FEBRUARY MORNING, COLD ENOUGH to numb gloveless fingers. The sky was grey, but with a hint of hopeful blue on the horizon. Sabre was commanded to wait once they reached the end of the lane. The dog watched Robbie venture on alone, its brown eyes forlorn.

Robbie moved carefully to the left and right, stepping over the puddles and muddiest parts of the path. It was always like this when it'd been raining all night, making progress a messy and noisy splashfest. At the end of this lane was Green Edge

– weer the coloureds live –

where the family from Ghana lived in the big old house that used to be Potter's farm. They had a posh car that didn't break down all the time, unlike his dad's patched-up wreck with the farting exhaust.

The Ghana family's dad, Mr Nimo, had taken over as the science teacher at Robbie's school. Robbie didn't think Mr Nimo liked him. Last week, he'd told Robbie off in front of the class for not paying attention. Everyone laughed. Robbie had the smallest labcoat on – it was the only one left when he got to school late because Dad's car had trouble starting again. Robbie had stood there, looking silly with the white sleeves too short and the coat too tight to fasten the buttons properly. A scarecrow for everyone's amusement.

He hated science.

"One two, buckle my shoe. Three four, lock yer door," he sang to himself.

Most of the kids from school would be in town today. But not *all*.

Make yerself useful, get rid of some of the mess rind this place.

He adjusted the rifle bag, which slipped loose over time. Once he got near the Nimos' land he could head into the treeline and sneak to the back of the house.

The puddles further down this sloping lane grew in number where the path had eroded, water washing stones out of place and making the surface more and more irregular, as if it tried to become a stream. To become something greater than its parts. In some places, at the edge of the path, the water succeeded, and gurgled in muddy rivulets.

The lane curved to the right here, around a steep bank of clumped grass with collapsed fencing at the base. As he followed the bend two dark-skinned figures appeared ahead and his heart skipped a beat. He looked back up the lane, about to disappear, but an enthusiastic cry of "Hey, Robbie!" proved he'd already been seen. He stopped. Loosened the straps so that the bag hung lower on his back, wasn't so obviously a gun.

"Robbie Robbie Robbie!" said Kwesi with a wide toothy smile as he approached. Next to him was his sister, Obaa Yaa. She was in the year below Robbie at school; Kwesi was in his class. Obaa Yaa dropped a step behind her brother and smiled shyly at Robbie.

"Don't wear my name ite," Robbie said.

"You are so funny! Always funny in school!"

"Yeah, the best clown in town."

Kwesi held his hand out, an action that always seemed to give him pleasure. They shook, then squeezed hard, each trying to crush the other's fingers. Kwesi broke off first, laughing. "You win!" He turned to his sister. "Grip of steel!" he explained. "I can never beat him!"

"I pay fer it. Won't be able to write fer a week." Robbie shook out his hand in mock pain. "Gets me ite of homework, though."

"Ha ha!" Kwesi peeked around Robbie. "What is that?" he asked, pointing at the bag.

"A gun."

His eyes widened. "You allowed a *gun*?"

"Aye."

"For what purpose?"

"Shooting. Animals 'n' stuff."

Kwesi whistled. Robbie liked the look of respect on his face, and was about to boast when he noticed Obaa Yaa was frowning at him.

"Shooting is killing," she said, with quiet firmness.

"But it's not mine, it's my dad's," Robbie backtracked. "I don't use it really. I were jost taking it to him today."

"Can I see?" Kwesi asked.

"No!" his sister snapped. "Leave it alone!"

Robbie shook his head. "Yaa's rate." At the sad look on Kwesi's face he added, "Maybe another time."

"Yes. I would like that," he said. "Hey, Robbie, we're going on to the village. A walk. Do you want to come with us?"

Kwesi had new jeans on. A bulge in his pocket where he carried his iPhone. Obaa Yaa wore a long skirt, and had somehow avoided splashing mud around the hem. Whereas Robbie knew what he looked like. Frayed camo trousers. A hoodie with a tear in the sleeve. Boots with a hole forming near the little toe.

"I can't." Robbie gestured at his gun bag.

"No problem. See you soon." Kwesi wasn't put out. He clapped Robbie on the shoulder and walked on with his sister, humming a song Robbie didn't recognise. He watched after them, hoping Obaa Yaa would turn back and wave or smile. She didn't.

If he wanted new things he had to seize them for himself.

OBAA YAA WAS DIFFERENT WHEN she was alone with him. She didn't go quiet. Robbie wasn't subdued either. It was the presence of other people that ruined things.

Some weeks ago he'd been passing over their land, swishing a stick at long grass as he walked, fantasising about a zombie apocalypse; she had appeared from behind a tree, absorbed in something on her phone. They'd both been startled for a few beats by the sudden arrival.

"What are you doing here?" she asked.

"Going up to the fields. See the snowdrops."

"Snowdrops?"

"Flowers." He bit his lip but she didn't laugh at him. Her wide eyes just seemed interested. "Want to come?" he asked, surprising himself. The fact that she nodded surprised him even more.

He'd shown her the place where snowdrops were spreading under a hedge. Still only green spears, but soon the white would break. And nearby was another flower. It was also closed, but a hint of yellow existed in that bent-over bud, making the stalk look like a green streetlight.

"You like daffodils?" he asked.

"Yes, but I have never seen a real one. Only picture." Then she laughed. It was a sweet sound, over too soon. "I learnt the poem at school in Ghana, 'I wandered lonely as a cloud,' William Wordsworth. I did not understand all of it. I thought daffodil would look like clouds. I was surprised when I saw a picture of one, like a yellow trumpet."

"Bend dine, look here."

"Bend dine?"

"Down."

She nodded, crouched next to him and he showed her the flower head.

"See? Yellow. Come back here and check it, you'll see it open soon enough. Next week, maybe."

"I will! I would like to touch one." Her hair was tightly braided in an intricate pattern, and he caught a floral whiff of coconut as they leaned in together.

"Hey, I know, I'll show you a real good patch," he said. "Weer theer will be loads of 'em."

"A host of dancing daffodils!"

"Well, wobbling ones."

She touched him gently on his arm as she stood. Such a slight touch, but, like a splinter, he was aware of that spot for days afterwards.

"What does Robbie mean?" she asked as they walked on.

"Huh?"

"I thought names usually had some other meaning here? Like Carl means Prince Charles?"

"Maybe it means I come from a family of thieves." She looked confused. "Robbers?" he added.

"That is a joke? Robbie Robber?"

"Yeah, it is a joke. Dun't mean owt, really. Jost a name. Like Robbie Williams."

"Robbie Williams?"

"Never mind. Whut does yer name mean? Something special?"

She shook her head, smiling. "It means I was born on a Thursday."

"Fer real?"

"Yes. That is how we get names in Ghana. Kwesi means 'boy born on a Sunday'. Mother is called Abena, a woman born on a Tuesday."

"Wow. That's simpler. Better on the kid. They won't get bullied then fer being called Calvin, or Nathaniel."

As they walked he noticed she was graceful, didn't clomp like him. He could imagine she was a princess back in Ghana. Her country was a mystery to him. Maybe they'd have a book on it in the library. He should go before it shut down forever and knowledge became an extra bus ride away.

STOP LOOKIN' AT FUCKIN' PLANTS you useless lump.

He woke from the memory, and his smile faded.

All jost going to waste now Potter's dead.

No. It was not a waste.

Once he'd left the path up to Bradnop's Brook the going got muddier. Things were less churned up and shitty now the cows were gone, but he was still surprised by how splattered his combat trousers were. No matter how careful he was, mud got everywhere. Maybe it'd add to the camouflage.

He skirted one of the fields, climbed through a gap in the barbed-wire fence, and made his way behind the old cow sheds. He peeped in. Light speared from rusty holes in the corrugated roof (Potter never had looked after things). It was so quiet now, without the cows lowing. He could hear the birds instead. He had a quick cig and just listened. Smoke drifted up from his mouth like a dragon's, fading into the air before it reached the tin roof.

After flicking away the butt he left the sheds behind and cut through treacherous rough ground below the last line of trees, a mix of lofty ash and spiky holly. The gun seemed heavier on his shoulder, strap cutting in like a prodding finger.

He scuttled down a steep embankment on his arse, and was at last in sight of the pond. It had grown in the recent rains, maybe even counted as a lake now. You'd be able to swim in it if you could put up with the sucking mud on the way in and out, punctuated by waterlogged trees and brambles. The mid-ranges were the terrain of long grass and reeds, marshy ground that was difficult to trek across. He kept his distance from the pond, crouched low, and paralleled it as he made his way to where he'd spotted the ducks, even though the chances of seeing them again were low.

Ducks had sharp eyesight, especially for any movement that could represent a predator. He moved from bush to prickly bush; hillock to grassy clump; and was soon near the overgrown areas of spiny reed heads sprouting from the water, where the ducks had fed a few days ago. Nearby was a fallen tree, rotten to the core, which would make a good hide. He belly crawled the last ten metres, commando-like, over open ground that smelt of gassy rotting plant matter. Cold water squelched up, soaking his arms and body and legs. All in all it was a pretty miserable business.

He sat with his back to the tree. Black slimy mould patches spread where it pushed into the squidgy earth, and exposed bits of wood crumbled away at the touch, sending insects scurrying for cover. Robbie leaned the gun bag against the log and removed a small pair of field binoculars from his jacket's front pocket. After slowly raising his head above the top of the log he rolled the focus dial with his forefinger until he had a clear, black-framed view of the expansive reedy area further up, looking for tell-tale signs.

The water was cloudy brown in one patch, as if mud had been churned up. He focussed on that area and saw movement amongst the stalks, but after a few patient minutes he concluded it had just been the breeze.

He scanned to the other side, wishing he knew more about this. Did he need some kind of call? Decoys?

Dead foliage in a tangle. Then a ripple in the water. Just another distraction.

But ... no. *Something*.

A duck appeared from the thick vegetation. Muddy brown plumage and a dark cap. Large head and bill. White cheek. It dived, disappearing below the surface which reflected grey sky, presumably feeding as it swam along the sludgy bottom.

And then another appeared, tail twitching, head turning warily. More movement behind.

He peeped over the top of the binoculars. The ducks were close enough that he could see them clearly with his naked eyes. He had really good eyesight. The optician told him. Robbie was proud of that. Something he did well. If you see things, and know how to interpret them, and remember them, then it was a kind of power.

After lowering himself back down behind the log, Robbie slid the gun from its bag, revealed the break-action of the old twelve-gauge shotgun and loaded a red plastic cartridge of steel shot into each breech, before quietly closing and latching it.

The way Obaa Yaa looked when she saw his gun ... so different to how she had looked at him when he showed her daffodils.

The closely grouped birds hadn't seen him. Six of them. Six out of the twenty that remained in the country. He could earn a fortune. That was what he needed to focus on. Money. To get buses whenever he wanted. To dress well. To impress her. To make her family like him.

He lifted the gun, rested his left arm on the log, holding the fore-end stable. The scratched wooden stock was snug against his shoulder as he leaned his cheek on it and lined up the sights. Thirty metres was pushing his accuracy but he only needed to hit one. Any others were a bonus. And he could get off two shots. With luck the birds might panic and dive rather than fly off, giving time to reload, maybe wade in nearer through the waist-deep icy water, get another chance at closer range.

He tracked the birds smoothly as they swam and dived and preened. They obviously felt safe here. Their home. Two were females, recognisable by the dark horizontal bar across their white cheeks. Nothing flash in their plumage, but he empathised. They were the kind of bird he'd be, rather than something striking like a kingfisher or chaffinch. It would be interesting to see them in the summer, when the males went all chestnut and developed bright blue bills, like sky on the clearest days, that colour which seems to go on and on forever, infinite potential.

He flipped the safety off and tried to still his breathing but his heart wouldn't comply, it hammered strangely in his chest.

The ruddy ducks mated with the white-headed ducks, the article said. In biology he remembered that if things could mate and have fertile offspring then they were the same species. Just different appearances. Why were the RSPB and conservationists so keen to keep things segregated? Mrs Cooper at school again, in her history lessons. Robbie had learnt the word *eugenics*. Yet the kids were told that was a *bad* thing.

He put his finger on the trigger, inhaled through his nostrils, taking in the dank, marshy scents. Ready for a long, slow exhale when he fired. And yet his forehead prickled as sweat broke out and instantly chilled.

It didn't matter to the birds if their partners looked different.

He gritted his teeth. Pulled a fraction more. His eyes were moistening, the mist getting into them, clammy and all-pervading. Things blurred. His good eyesight was letting him down.

Obaa Yaa seemed like a good person. She made him want to be better too.

He squeezed the trigger but his finger froze. Wouldn't tighten any more.

After swallowing hard past some obstruction in his throat he lowered the gun with shaking arms, put the safety back on, and leaned it against the tree trunk. He scanned the marshy land, the drifting mists that hid mysteries, turning normal outlines into ominous and magical shapes. It was a surreal place. More so as it reverted to peace now that Potter and his family and his tractors and quad bikes were gone. You could believe in things again.

"Tiddy Mun," he whispered.

Tiddy Mun, the small bog spirit. An old grey man wreathed in mist whose creepy laughter was said to resemble the call of the peewit. This was his land. Isolated, damp, quiet.

Robbie took his penknife from a side pocket in his cargo pants. He kept it sharp. No rust on its blade. Robbie squeezed his eyes shut and put the edge against the pad of his thumb. A quick slide, a sharp slice, and it was over. He kept his eyes shut and let his thumb drip, imagined the red droplets sinking into the mud.

"Tiddy Mun, Tiddy Mun, I offer a pact to ya. I'll leave the ducks alive. In exchange – let her like me. That's all."

He stuck his stinging thumb in his mouth and sucked the coppery blood as he opened his eyes. Some said you shouldn't contract with spirits because they were slippery word-twisters, but what did the cowards know? It was a sealed deal. The lonely marshland around him remained creepily quiet but beautiful, and Robbie half-expected to see a small grey figure slink into some reeds.

THE SOUR SMELL OF PIGSHIT, the frightened squeals. It was the farm all right. Robbie squelched through stinking mud, somehow dirtier-feeling than what he'd experienced at the pond, and slid back the heavy door to the first shed with a grating squeal. Flies flew past him out of the rancid heat that hit like a wave of gas. It was the farrowing shed. Sows held down by metal bars so they couldn't move, lay on slats that let the shit and piss fall into channels below. Baby porkers fought over the teats. But his dad wasn't there. He dragged the door shut with an effort, the rails screeching almost as much as the pigs.

He was crossing the yard to the other sheds when a nearby door banged and his dad emerged with Fappy. Dad whistled and looked happy. Robbie wondered what was wrong with him. They splatted their way over to Robbie. Fappy had high wellies and a dirty green overcoat on. His shaggy black hair was stuck up as if he'd been sweating and had run fingers through it. His hands were shoved deep into coverall pockets.

"Owe rate?" Fappy asked.

"Owe rate," Robbie replied.

"Whut dust want?" asked his dad.

"Brought you this." Robbie unslung the heavy gun bag and handed it to his dad.

"Whut fer?"

"Fer pig wi' brock leg."

Fappy and his dad looked at each other. His dad's bushy eyebrows bunched up.

"No need. Sorted now," Fappy said, with a sly grin. There were dark marks on his clothes. They could be slurry. Or something else.

"Don't worry, it warrant a pregnant one," his dad said.

"That's not why 'is face dropped, is it?" Fappy noted. "'E's nesh, yer lad. But I'll get it ite of him. He can give me a hand wi' the castration. Snap off those bollocks." Fappy gestured pulling something imaginary and elastic, then made a clicking noise with his tongue. He grinned all the time. "One o' the sows is due to shoot pink uns ite this afternoon. Do it rate off."

That set Fappy and his dad laughing. They were so fucking hilarious.

"Ey, 'fore I forget, and talkin' of balls, yer dad were telling me it's yer birthday next weekend. I can get you a football. Not new, but good enough." When Robbie didn't reply straight away Fappy shrugged and added, "That's if you still kick 'em rind, not too big fer it now yer playin' wi' guns."

"I still play footie a bit." Then an idea. The coach always said *When you see an opening you should seize it right off.* "Just not on the school team," Robbie added.

"I thought you woz good?"

"Am allrate. But a lad in class, mar mate, beat me onto the lineup."

"Which mate?"

"Kwesi. E's good."

His dad and Fappy looked at each other.

"*Really* good," Robbie added, getting their attention back. "I could start practising with 'im, get better, get on the team."

"Oh aye? Does 'e live on Potter's? One o' the black uns?" asked Fappy.

"They live at Green Edge."

"Runnin' round's in theer blood. Weer wost they drug up?"

"Ghana. They're from Ghana."

"That weer we get bananas from?" Fappy asked, laughing.

"They're smarter than you. Kwesi's dad's a scientist. Teaches me."

"That rate?" Fappy's smile faded. "Superstition dun't go wi' science, I know that. And they can't even speak proper, let alone teach."

"E's a good teacher."

"You should stick wi' your sort."

"Kwesi *is* my sort. And I really want to get on the team. If I play with 'im, it'd help."

Fappy snorted. "Well I'll think on abite yer present." He scratched his nose with a dark-stained finger. "A voodoo doll or something," he muttered.

"Come on. Let's go back fer tea," Robbie's dad interrupted.

Robbie and Fappy stared at each other but Robbie could never face that blank hardness for long. Robbie broke the eye duel and left with his dad.

THE RAIN HAD BEEN AND gone. Now it was a proper cold spell. Robbie dragged his chair next to the electric heater, made sure all the bars were on, and carried on eating his cornflakes before they sogged up.

"Happy birthday," Dad said, coming into the kitchen in his dressing gown. He held out a card and a present which was badly wrapped in paper left over from Christmas.

Robbie put the card and bowl to one side and tore away at the snowmen. Too small for trainers, too light for books. CDs?

The paper gave way to a box. A phone box. A HTC phone box. *A smart phone.*

His mouth opened but no sound came out.

No, it had to be just a box, a cruel trick; inside would be a big Mars bar or something, like last year ...

"It's charged. Credit on it too," his dad said with a laugh as Robbie held the light thing that was mostly screen – *mostly screen!* – in his hand reverently.

"You won on the horses?"

"Nah. But we can afford a bit of luxury sometimes. Oh, and theer's a football off Fappy in the boot of the car. He said you'll be on the team before yer know it."

A phone. A really nice one. Better'n some of the other kids had.

"Thanks! This is brilliant!"

That's it. Things would change. The Tiddy Mun pact was working.

PLAN. SMART PEOPLE HAD PLANS. And he was now one of the smart people.

He would go to Green Edge. Tell Kwesi and Obaa Yaa that it was his birthday. Show his phone, give his number, get theirs. Go for a walk to the village, all three of them. In the future they could message each other. And if he and Obaa Yaa sent texts to each other, no one else would know.

It was perfect.

He took a hurried shower, lathering with so much shampoo it stung his eyes, then put clean clothes on. His best clothes, in fact: the trainers that were still in good shape and hadn't been worn since they'd been in the washing machine. He combed his hair, pulling at knotty tangles, wondering if he should get Mrs Broughton to cut it. Maybe tomorrow.

Outside was icy freshness as the breeze caressed his just-washed face. He began to sprint, windchill competing with the inner warmth from activity. He didn't care which one won; he was happy, light, leaping over sludgy areas like Superman.

He stopped, out of breath, hands on knees, smiling and panting. Near his feet was an area of white frost yet untouched by morning sunlight. When he looked closely he could see the feathery crystals that glittered. Beauty up close, seen with his good eyes, all the world precious, down to the smallest.

Their car was in the drive. It was clearly a posh car since it wasn't splattered in shit. Some sort of new-looking Volvo. He let his fingers caress the bonnet as he passed. This sign told him the family were home.

He checked his reflection in the front door's small pane of glass and brushed his tangled fringe back with a licked palm. He tried a smile, but it looked unusual on his face. Best to just stick to politeness. He knocked.

After a long wait he knocked again, harder, and then heavy footsteps came down the hall. The rattle of a chain being removed, a key turned, the door only opened part way.

"Hello, Mr Nimo."

"What do you want?" the teacher snapped.

"Erm ... Please can I speak to Kwesi and Obaa Yaa?"

"No you cannot!" His voice was sharp, his expression fierce, and Robbie flinched. Mr Nimo was not normally like this.

Think quick.

"Am sorry abite the last class." Robbie had been caught toasting biscuits over a bunsen burner. "I won't do it again."

"I do not care about that."

Shouting came from within the house. Robbie didn't understand the words, then realised it must be Ghanaian. It sounded like Mrs Nimo. Anger in that voice too. Ah. He'd interrupted an argument.

Through the gap he saw her. She looked like she'd been crying. "Savages!" she said before disappearing from sight again. Was that a word from Ghana that just happened to sound like an English one?

"Go," said Mr Nimo, closing the door.

This wasn't right. Not what he'd *planned*.

Robbie put his foot forward. The door thumped into it, couldn't close. "Wait a second!"

Mr Nimo tried to shove the door harder. It hurt Robbie's foot, the trainers gave no crush protection, but he didn't budge.

"Please ... whut's wrong?" Robbie asked.

"Kwesi was attacked last night in the dark. Beaten with some kind of stick. One of his legs is broken. Satisfied?"

Robbie stopped resisting. The door slammed in his face.

After frowning at the painted wood for a few seconds Robbie turned and walked off. It was so shivery cold. Every exhale cast a grey foggy veil over what lay below his eyes. *Greyness. Mist.* A memory stirred.

This wasn't how it was supposed to be.

He looked at the phone in his hand.

He started to run.

THE GROUND WAS SO HARD-FROZEN he could pound over the muddy areas, they crunched rather than sucked. The grass was grey where frost still clung. He arrived breathless, taking big gulps of air, but without the freed happiness that normally suffused him after running. The pond was still, misty, mysterious. Not frozen over, but no doubt freezing.

He waded in without hesitation, gasping as the cold shock reached higher. It was worst when it got to his testicles, shrinking everything, numbing all but his mind, the mind that planned and could see so far, right to the bottom line. He fought to control his shuddering breathing when the water reached his midriff. Clean clothes now soaked with pond water but he didn't care. He had to know.

Robbie was a superhero. He could add things together and see the truth.

Into channels of water like navigable moats amongst the same reeds he'd recently spied on from a distance, looking for signs, dreading signs, his arms raised as if he was trying to scare a child by pretending to be a grey ghost. It looked as he'd expect. Maybe they were just away. The water resisted him but he pushed on, slipped on a slimy rock, almost fell, grabbed on to reeds and righted himself. His skin was now frozen tightness, and it spread, he couldn't stay in here much longer.

Dad was in a good mood.

Some reeds were shredded. He looked more closely. Jagged edges. A neatly punched hole in one tall leaf. And dried blood, near a blasted area. A reddened feather stuck between reeds.

Dad had taken the newspaper.

It was all blown apart. His fault. The reeds. The plans. Hope that other people could get along, see things properly, read the bottom line and understand. But no one else in this pig-shitting world could see it.

"Am sorry," he said aloud, words a sob, and wiped his eyes on his sleeve.

Then Robbie removed the phone from his jacket's inner pocket. There seemed nowt smart about it now. Everything was ruined.

Vermin on the ponds.

"Get ite of my brainpan you old bastard!" Robbie shouted.

He reached back to throw the blood-cursed phone as far away as possible; fool to think it could be part of life for someone like him. He could see it tumbling through the air, to plop in the muddy water and sink forever. The only revenge he'd get. Maybe enough of a sacrifice to placate Tiddy Mun, make things right. His arm swung forward, but at the last moment he tightened his grip and let his arm fall whilst still holding the phone.

No. *No!* You can't let bad uns win. They win too often. The world was twisted.

Not this time.

ROBBIE KNOCKED INSISTENTLY ON THE door. They'd shouted that he should go away, but he kept rapping even though his knuckles were sore. It was clear he would never stop; and eventually the door swept open angrily. Robbie spoke first.

"Am here because I'm Kwesi's friend. A real friend. And I just called the police. They'll be here soon." He thought about the cursed football. He didn't know what would happen tomorrow, but he could see as far as today, and he could see what was right. "And I'll tell 'em who did it."

Balance

"CALLIA, OVER HERE!"

"Lower your voice, Nerine, it is not seemly to hiss like the cobra."

Nerine grinned, ever the outspoken one. Her too-lively demeanour occasionally led her friends to worry for her. It was imprudent for a woman to attract too much attention to herself.

"Sorry, Callia." Nerine bowed her head, dark curly hair bobbing. She seemed so eager to pass on her news that she could not restrain her excitement.

Callia glanced around the cloistered courtyard. In the shade of an awning another pair of female slaves prepared a salad of cucumbers and rice. Callia wished that had been her assigned task for the morning. She loved the pungent aroma of garlic crushed between stones so that the pulp and juice ran into a bowl, mixing with the smooth oil and freshly squeezed lemon juice that would dress the food.

Nerine gripped the sleeve of Callia's pirahan and pulled her into the shade of the colonnade, out of the merciless sun.

"You make us look suspicious, sneaking in shadows to share whispered words," chided Callia.

"Yes, I know, but I wanted to tell you. I overheard the doctor. The Master is more sick than was thought, and is not long for this world."

Callia's pulse quickened, but she did not let any sign reach her face. "That is sad news, not something to grin about."

"There is more. Master has asked for you. I was sent to tell you because the Mistress would not. Why is this?"

"It is not your business, and you must learn to use your wide eyes more, and your poking nose and squeaking mouth less. If Master is truly on his deathbed then he may wish to discuss the future."

"You mean, whether there will be a new Master to replace him, or if we will all be split up and sent away?"

"Yes."

"And he wants to see you particularly because you have served him well?"

"I do not like that sly glint in your eyes, Nerine. I do not wish to see it again. If you behaved with half this impudence in front of the Mistress you would have been flogged."

"But you are not the Mistress. You are Callia."

Callia frowned. "I go now. Balance be with you."

"And with you, Callia."

CALLIA WAITED RESPECTFULLY, HEAD BOWED, as the three ephors filed out of the Master's chambers. The wise men were rarely seen but always had to be treated with the utmost honour. They were dressed in the traditional long brown linen tunic of a man, but with dark purple woollen cloaks over one shoulder to distinguish their rank. Although they moved quietly in their soft shoes they smelt strongly of coffee and cardamom, and Callia thought she would have sensed them even in the dark of a starless desert night.

She was surprised from her thoughts when one of them addressed her. Ephors were normally cold and silent in the presence of a woman.

"Balance be with you," he said, and she looked into his brown lined face, at eyes that seemed ancient. His beard was long and dark, and she sensed a certain unexplainable sadness in his expression.

"Balance be with you, Masters," she replied.

BEFORE SHE ENTERED THE ROOM she checked that she was presentable. Her pirahan was clean, a cream yellow, with long sleeves and cuts that ran up the sides from the waist. Below that her daman covered her legs down to her bare feet. Her nails were unpainted, for it was forbidden for slaves to use decoration. Her hair hung loose past her brown shoulders, glossy and black; like a thoroughbred's mane, the Master had sometimes joked.

She pushed through the rattling bead curtain. The Master's room was dark and still, with silk drapes over the narrow slit windows. But it was hot, despite the thick walls that kept out most of the sun's heat.

"Master?" Her eyes slowly adjusted to the gloom.

"Callia. Good. Open the windscoop. I am stifled."

She moved over to it, skirting a pile of embroidered cushions spread across the floor. As she raised the opening a breeze cooled her face, a breeze that had travelled free across the dunes before blowing into a hole at the top of the parapet wall where the windspeed was greatest, and being funnelled down to become a fellow prisoner in the room. There was spice in the air.

"Sit." He patted a cushion by the low bed.

His white tunic lay open. He had lost a great amount of weight – it hung like a loose fold of skin, making him seem smaller somehow.

She knelt by him. His eyes were on her but she did not meet his gaze directly. A bowl of millet, boiled into porridge, sat on a low table nearby. "Would you like me to feed you, Master?"

"No. You have heard the rumours, no doubt. That I am to die."

"Yes."

"They are true."

She did not reply, but did look into his face. It was so changed. His beard had been shaved but instead of making him look younger it revealed the unhealthy colour and lines of sickness underneath. Pain, even. Only his voice still belonged to the man she knew.

"I see you are not surprised. That is well. It has been a long time since we were alone. Too long, perhaps, I think, when I see your eyes like the desert night, and your caramel skin." His fingertips brushed her chin, raising it. "Beautiful." He sighed, long and low. "But now is not the time, nor will it ever come again, I fear." His hand fell back to the sheet, as if he was too tired to support it. "It is a shame how you were born, Callia. You should have been a princess. But we must not question the decisions of Gods. They are just to be acted upon."

"Is there really no hope, Master?"

"No. But I am resigned. You are good, Callia, are you not? You respect our traditions, and live as is expected of you. Even when we may secretly question the rightness of some of the strictures, in our secret minds, we cannot speak what we read there. Our culture is strict, and because we survive through it, we must go along with it. At one time I felt that I could read your secret mind, some parts of it, and it contained these questions too. *Why?* you might ask. *Why is the world this way?* But you control your thoughts. You have the strength of a man in many ways. That is not why I hold you in such esteem, but it is noble nonetheless."

"As we all do, I obey the laws, and obey you."

"Yes. And you must prepare for my passing, when you will move on after."

The room was filled with just light and shade and voice, it did not seem real any more, no weight to anything. A change, like a change in the wind perhaps, something altered. Possibly a different future.

"May I ask what will happen to me, Master? Will I serve the Mistress, or will I go to a new master?"

"Not a new master, but neither will it be the Mistress. One you know."

She wondered who he might mean: riddles and being cryptic were prized values in their culture, but it did not mean she could penetrate what men really meant. Possibly no woman could. She just accepted his words with a nod.

He asked her to recite a poem, and she did her best to make *The Weighing of the Heart* pleasing to his ear: but soon his breathing changed, and she slipped out of the room.

The Mistress was outside, sat on a cushioned bench, sewing. Although she wore the dark veil of sadness, *mikha ashwanti*, over her mouth and nose, her haunted eyes watched Callia sharply and without compassion. Callia bowed her head respectfully and moved away.

Had the Mistress listened to their conversation? It would not matter. Everyone knew that the Master had shown Callia favour in the past. It was one of the reasons why Callia was regarded as senior to the other slaves, but meant that from the Mistress there had only ever been coldness.

Such was life. You gain with one hand, but the sand slips through the fingers of the other, and you finish as you started: for all must even out in the end.

FOUR SUNS ON. IT SEEMED an age before this day was done. Callia had helped prepare food for the visiting ephors, days away from the nearest large town and therefore staying on the estate. Only the best would do for them. She had spent so long rolling meat dumplings infused with chilli and vinegar that by the time they were baked she would not have wanted to eat one, even if slaves had been allowed to eat meat. While they cooked she had to monitor the saleeg, careful that the rice and milk cooked together into a solid mix without burning. Someone else had then taken over, serving it with butter and poached meat sprinkled on top.

At last the slaves had been able to prepare and eat their own, simpler, meal before retiring. During the hottest periods some of the luckier workers were allowed to sleep on the flat roof of one of the adobe buildings, and now she stood at the crenellated parapet wall of the roof and watched the burning sun sink into its hazy red bed on the horizon, allowing the cool desert night to move in. She swallowed up and stored the beauty and peace of the scene using every sense: the many colours smeared across the sky, the fresh smell of olive oil from her meal, the soothing whirr of flying insects and the coolness of the patch of wind-blown sand beneath the soles of her feet. These things were memories that she would recall when doing mundane tasks, but for them to live in her mind she had to give herself fully to those sensations.

Tonight she was distracted, though. Questions nagged at her mind, to which she had no answers. Questions about the world. Had it always been like this, or were things somehow different in the past? And what lay over the horizon where the sun slept? She was imagining different places when Nerine rose from her date palm bedding and stood beside her.

"You often gaze into the sunset, Callia. What is it you see?"

"It is beautiful, but I see no more than you. The horizon, somewhere I would love to visit."

"It is just desert, isn't it? On and on forever, beyond the last town. I hear that none who venture there ever return."

"Maybe because they find what they look for, and don't want to come back."

They spoke quietly so as not to disturb the other slaves who slept on their own mats.

"I was in the village today, Callia, and overheard some things. And before you stab me with your tongue, I did as you told me to – I used my eyes and ears, not my poking nose or squeaking mouth."

Callia smiled. "Very good, Nerine. I think that your mind will be as sharp as my tongue one day."

Information was hard to come by. They were told only as much as they needed to know. Many of the slaves never even saw the nearest town; those entrusted with going to other settlements had little chance to gossip with the women there, since men always watched over them. Callia had been to nearby Horis a handful of times, and always savoured the adventure. Of the world beyond she knew nothing, but prayed that one day she would experience it.

"They are building a great stone mausoleum on the dusty plains. Beyond the high rocks, there." Nerine pointed towards a dark shadow at the edge of the estate, past the palm trees and well, only just visible in the last of the light. "Many slaves are forced to labour on it. I pity them. It must be hard work."

It was rumoured that slave women who were stronger or less attractive than the rest were worked to death in construction projects. Callia did not like to believe in such tales.

"Who did you hear this from?"

"Our overseer was talking to a man in the market while I selected spices. I pretended not to listen, and heard that much before they noticed me and moved away. The mausoleum suggests that they are all prepared for the Master to die."

"They are. The Master told me himself. He said we must prepare also."

"The Mistress is unhappy. She snaps if things are not perfect. At first I thought it was because she will lose her husband, but I wonder if it is something more. Mistress knows things we do not. I wish I was a Mistress."

Callia glanced around. None of the shapes on their bedrolls stirred.

"Be careful what you say, Nerine," she whispered.

The sun was gone now, the sky and land all dark and indistinguishable as night clouds blocked out the starlight but kept them warm.

"We must sleep," Callia added. Then, in a surprising impulse, she put her arms around Nerine and gave her a quick hug. For one moment, in the dark, she imagined that Nerine was the child she had never met: the girl she bore from the Master, taken from her before a week had passed, presumably as a gift to the Master of some other estate. There were rumours of what happened to female slave children, but her stomach knotted at the thought ... No, they could not be true.

Then she wrapped herself in a linen sheet, and fell asleep fantasising of happier things. Callia had a daughter who had been freed, and had gone on to become a princess.

THE NEXT DAY ONE OF the men told them that the Master had died and they were all to be in mourning until the new moon. Some of the slaves wept. Callia did not.

A ceremony would take place, a symbolic joining made holy by the ephors. Only those slaves most favoured were to attend, and then they would be moved on, not to return to this estate.

That afternoon Callia was approached by one of the ephors. It was not the one with the old and sad eyes, but one who seemed to dislike the task of speaking to her. She was told that she was the first to be chosen of the ten most favoured, and was to be at the ceremony, and she should be honoured.

She thanked the ephor in formal terms, head bowed, but in her heart was turmoil. She would be leaving the estate at last, and the thought of it filled her with excitement. Would things be different in her new home? Might she be moved to the town? Might she even one day meet her own daughter – who would now be waist-high – and give her the mother's love she deserved? After all, Callia was favoured: that had been recognised, and if the world was a logical one, that fact must lead to reward.

She would be sad to leave Nerine. She considered for one mad moment having the impudence to suggest that Nerine should also be favoured, and how she would justify the many reasons to the ephor. Callia imagined that the ephor would listen coldly but discuss it with the others and finally agree, and Nerine would follow her into a new life. She considered all that but said nothing. She was not sure why she let the ephor just walk away. Maybe it was because she could not be sure that she would be making Nerine's lot better, and would hate to think that Nerine might be forced to give up a position in the Mistress's inner circle of servants to move on to something that may not be an improvement, just for the sake of Callia's loneliness.

No, the possibility that Nerine would come to despise her for it was not good. Let her stay in her position. Her prospects were decent if she stayed modest. That thought made Callia happy.

NERINE WAS NOT TO BE at the ceremony – none but the men and the chosen ones were – but she helped Callia prepare. The ceremonial tunic was a fine white linen, and the favoured slaves were anointed with cinnamon bark scented oil. Nerine combed some of the oil through Callia's hair, whilst constantly chattering about her mysterious prospects: where Callia might go, who her new Master might be; and also about what might happen to Nerine on the estate, whether the Mistress would manage it alone or whether a new Master would move in. For once Callia let her run on in that childlike way. She did not want to chide her for anything when they might never meet again.

Solemn music drifted in through the narrow slits; men were playing the reed nay, its haunting fluted notes conjuring appropriate images of the wind blowing through rocks in holy places, and the wailing of those mourning the dead. Occasionally a bendir drum would beat, slow as dragging feet and a further call to join the procession.

Callia forced a smile for Nerine, whilst thinking of fitting words on which to part, and was surprised to see tears brimming in Nerine's eyes.

"I don't know why I am so sad, Callia, but I can't help it."

Nerine hugged Callia fiercely, and it numbed her heart to have to remove those arms as the procession passed the adobe. Words seemed pointless and feeble and incomplete; as with the lingering echo of the nay's music in the room, some things were better expressed without language. Callia wiped Nerine's eyes with her thumbs, then kissed her forehead. She stood and walked into the sunlight without looking back, and it took great effort to be strong in the leaving. Compassion and strength: they were the only things of value that she could leave with Nerine which might help her in whatever her future would be, and they would have to be gifts enough.

She joined the other slaves on their procession into the future.

THE ASSEMBLED GROUP STOOD ON the blistering sand under the scorching sun. Beyond them was the mausoleum of fresh sandstone blocks, decorated around the top with geometric patterns painted in red and black. The Master's body was inside – it was said that his spirit would be watching from the roof.

The chief ephor was dressed fully in purple robes, a hood casting his face into shadow so that only part of his dark beard could be clearly seen. The other ephors stood under a shading tarpaulin, heads bowed solemnly. No breeze flapped that fabric, the only movement of air being an unreal shimmer as it baked off the ground. Beyond them the male musicians had laid down their instruments so that pensive silence reigned.

Ten goats were tied in a line before the mausoleum while estate overseers watched over them, eyes alert but bodies frozen still as statues. To Callia's knowledge the estate had never been attacked by the rumoured bandits that roamed the deserts, but those outlaws were said to be the reason for the strong men who did not smile and who carried a sharp khukuri knife at their sides.

The ten slave girls were tied too, by the wrists, Callia at one end of the line, being the first chosen. The Mistress stood alone behind the slaves, hands also bound. Eleven women, surrounded by men, a reversal of the normal state of affairs when males were the outnumbered group.

Some aspects of the ceremony seemed familiar to Callia. Though she had never attended a funeral, she had seen girls being bound together before, when they came to the estate from elsewhere as new servants. It was symbolic of the tie to a new Master, in the same way that this was no doubt symbolic of the tie to the deceased. Some traditions were easy to interpret. Others were impenetrable without the knowledge that men kept to themselves.

Callia noted that a shallow trench had been dug in the earth before the ephors, separating them from women and goats. The world was full of such divisions.

The chief ephor began to chant in a language unknown to Callia. She felt that it was an older language because of the way the sounds echoed, something retrieved from the unknown past. Everyone stood still, despite the melting discomfort of searing sun, since it was a tenet of their culture that things should not change. She was so used to the same templates being passed down from generation to generation that it was difficult to even imagine how things could be done differently, what change would look and smell and feel like. Change would require breaking the balance, something seen as such a great and dangerous taboo that even to think of it was to flush one's cheeks with shame.

The words went on and on, possibly only understood by the ephors, a soporific drone that triggered introspection. However, Callia's thoughts were interrupted when guards led the goats towards the trench. Metal spiral hooks had been embedded into the rock before it, and at various points the ropes were wound around them so that the goats remained fixed in a line. Some did not like being moved so resisted, but it was futile, and soon all were fixed in place. Callia hoped it was not as she suspected, but two guards moved to the first goat. One forced it to lie down at the edge of the small trench and sat on its chest. It struggled but could not get back up, the man's weight on its ribs forcing out its air in a horrendous bellow which made the other goats pull fruitlessly against their ropes. The second guard drew his curved khukuri from the leather sheath at his side, gripped the goat's chin tight in one hand, then cut its throat. The blade was razor sharp, creating a huge gash from which the kicking goat's blood pumped as the guard made sure that it gushed into the gutter in front of the goat. The other goats smelt the blood and understood what was going on. They struggled and made heart-rending panicked noises, but they were held fast, increasing their terror.

The ephor now spoke in the common tongue. "To join the Master in eternal life, so he shall not want."

Callia had already looked away from the killing, sickened in her stomach. But she could not block out the horrible, frightened noises that made her think of a baby crying.

She always disliked sacrifices, had no stomach for it. She had only seen it a few times before, a single goat killed to honour the Gods at one of the festivals. It was always men who took the life, and mostly men who ate the meat, the woman's role being to cook it and serve it to them. On the rare occasions when an opportunity to eat meat arose, she usually declined, since she could not separate the thought of the animal's fear from the thing on a plate in front of her; whereas dates and figs and olives, and other produce of the earth, seemed more a product of life than death.

The men moved on to the next goat, which snorted as it struggled. The goats were seeing the others die, their blood being drained into a channel, not given the mercy of ignorance. It seemed to take minutes for each animal to cease its frantic and hopeless struggle, life clinging on for as long as possible. It would be forbidden to cover her ears, so all she could do was let her eyes fill with tears of pity. She was not alone in her sympathy, as a glance at the faces of some of her fellow favoured told her.

Another eight bleating goats to go. The ceremony would not continue forever: then a new life of some sort would begin, duties done and appropriate respect shown to the previous Master.

As each goat died its limp form was untied and wrapped in linen before being carried into the impenetrable dark rectangle of the mausoleum. She knew that at the end of the ceremony the doorway would be sealed forever to protect the Master's body from the corrosive desert sands and the preying jackal.

The ephor proclaimed that the blood was to feed the earth, but she had not heard all of what was said, trying to retreat from the ordeal to the calm place in her mind which was a perpetual sunset of calming hope.

It seemed an age before the din of horror was over and the final goat's lone cry in the wilderness ceased. The two executioners were splashed with blood, hazy red beads on their faces and hands mired in gore.

Then the ephor announced that the women were to move to the trench for the end of the ceremony. He said it was symbolic, and they should not be alarmed.

None of the girls moved at first, just glanced at each other nervously, but when some of the armed men approached they began to walk slowly. It was just a symbol; a gesture of respect and ownership, however gruesome the scene. *Only symbolic,* she thought, surreptitiously testing the tightness of the fine rope around her wrists and surprised at its resistance. The symbolic tie she had seen in joining ceremonies fell apart at the slightest pull after the bondage ceremony was over; these knots were different, tight and cutting. Unnecessarily so, though perhaps funereal ceremonies required more, in the same way that the sacrifice of ten goats – not even to be used for food – showed the scale of this ceremony was greater than others.

As they reached the trench her stomach tightened to see the blood-soaked sand and dirt at the bottom, a clotted and darkening red so different from the ethereal beauty of the sunset skies of her dreams. A girl to her left struggled and tried to move away, but of course that was impossible. The ephor told them to be calm, the ceremony would soon be over and they could move on, just to kneel and be calm. Three men encouraged them to do so with firm grips, and they efficiently tied the ropes to the hoops. Callia looked at the other girls, sensing fear in their anxious glances to each other, but all still playing the part as they had been told, ingrained decorum and obeisance.

They were now all tied. The rank and rich metallic fluid smell from the pit in front sickened her. Even though she did not make the mistake of looking into it again, red smeared the edge of her vision.

The ephor was speech-making once more, referring to ancient civilisations that had shown the way. Her mind picked up some sense of it but would not settle or be calm. *They were being honoured.* Her gaze kept going back to the two blood-splashed guards, who still stood nearby: why had they not departed? Some of the girls sobbed. Callia noticed pristine linen in the pile which had been used to wrap the dead goats' bodies.

The wise Old Ones knew the true ways. The cloths preyed on her mind. *The history of our ancestors goes back twelve thousand years.* Time that could not be comprehended. *The honoured tribes of Sumerians, Egyptians, the Shang Dynasty, Mesopotamia.* She had heard of none of those. The two men with knives moved closer. *More recent ancestors who infected the under-earth with profane weapons and lost the balance.* She pulled experimentally at her bonds again, but they were tight. *Infernal Anglo-Americans and those in their thrall during the tear-birth of the Jugular Laek.*

Most of the girls were crying now, the rope tugged on her wrists as one struggled. *And the unleashed biolog-wickedness and chemical curses mean there are now few whole men born to the Earth, no balance except what men make for themselves, and Shining-eye Gods allow.* She could see that the girl next to her was trying to reach the hoop in the ground, to untie herself, but it was no good – moving hands to one hoop was impossible when it meant tightening the rope that was tied to the hoop on the other side. A balance that could not be broken by the person so tied. *But by appeasing penance and sacrifice the Old Ones may one day restore balance for the taut sliver of life clinging to the burning plains.* The two men with knives were now to the far left of the line, furthest from Callia. The girls struggled more, and wailed to wrench any beating heart. *Flaying winds and the long burn separate the true tribes, but we will crawl up and reunite.* Callia turned to her right, and gazed at the Mistress, tied behind them and crying also. *You were honoured to serve him in life, eternal.* The Mistress had no abhorrence for Callia, she now saw. Any hate had never been directed at her. She and the Mistress were at peace. *Do not struggle. You must understand our reasons, and agree. Only a brief opening, then your souls will pour free and be honoured forever in return.*

A piercing scream erupted from the other end of the line. The words of the ephor about being respectful and calm were just noise, the meaning behind them like a cruel blade hidden amongst fruit. Callia still refused to look to her left, tried to ignore the kicking and struggling of the girl at the edge of her vision, the men watching with hollow eyes. Nine girls to the left of her, she was last. Their screams echoed the ololuge, the ritual scream of sacrifice, and tore at her mind. The sunset, all she could do was focus on that, there could be no escape from this prison that she now saw was more a prison of words and minds than it was of ropes and estates, and there would be no end to the prison until the sun ceased to rise and set. Screaming and struggling, getting closer, her heart raced and she knew that to look would be to break her trance and she would not be able to stop from screaming herself, screaming out her loathing for all that this system was, and did, and thrived on ...

Movement to her right, the Mistress forced to kneel beside her. Callia would not have to suffer being the last, after all. They looked at each other, a mixed sandstorm of compassion and understanding and anger and trembling fear uniting them. Callia would not ever see her daughter alive again – if she even was alive – but it would be over soon, she could hear movement to her left, and for as long as possible she would look into the eyes of this woman to her right and extract as much courage as she could. This woman was not her Mistress, Callia saw that now. She was her sister.

Bloodline

BA-THOOM, BA-THOOM

the comforting beat of the blood under it all, always, the constant, the level everything else was measured by in wake and sleep that ebbed and flowed, recalling no past, no time before that measured pulse

ba-thoom, ba-thoom, ba-thoom

all was curled-up dreaming time in here, this hole, senses confined below a surface of soft tissue, unknown what lay beyond, unknown where the dreams came from, maybe shared from the soft shell

ba-thoom, ba-thoom

the deep vibration rhythm pulse was something other but the same, another beat, a muffled echo like all echoed in here, stronger but it added strength to little one, they were one in the wet and warm, the peace of safe and oneness

ba-thoom

and growling gurgles at times, from just outside this cocoon, so close, told it something of the protector, feelings, it knew hunger this way, it knew of tiredness, it knew of sickness, it knew of crying, it shared, it partook of the one outside, and little one wanted to share its peace sphere bubble with the big echo but knew not how

ba-thoom

and muffled noises from not-near sometimes, not just the one who blood-beat the same, but deep slow beyond-sounds, to-ing and fro-ing outside, more than echoes, rattling shrill noises not beat-pattern, not comfort-rhythm, reply noises to the lovely sound of the calming one

ba-thoom, ba-thoom

not so good then, best when floating in the dream-wake peace of the two beats alone

ba-thoom, ba-thoom, ba-thoom, ba-thoom

and worst the raucous and terrifying clatters and shouts beyond, the shouting was contraction, all pull in so tight

ba-thoom ba-thoom ba-thoom ba-thoom

deepest voice sound, angriest voice sound, and screaming and a hard slap noise that stops the scream and vibration heaves, fire retching that contracts and squeezes around so tight not protecting, but expelling

ba-thoomba-thoomba-thoomba-thoom

not happy, but hurting, cry, wobble as if off balance, cry, one feel other feel, not two but one, beat too fast, itwillbequick hurt not

kick

kick kick kick

.

.

.

.

kick

ba-thoom

but after the bad, many many many beats after, ba-thoom, ba-thoom, all quiet again when sob shakes fade, and now the comforting beat of the blood only, under it all, always, so can feel the gentle noises, hushing noises, this love pressure, whispered sweet nothings, push warm, the touch of the one it is part with, the one that is love, and that is also happy when they are alone, both feel it one experience, it somehow knows, and dreams come again, ebb and flow

ba-thoom

and somehow the sounds reach it and small one knows them loves them, because those sounds repeat in quietness many times, times before, times now, almost a third beat to join them, the sounds are this –

I love you and want so much to meet you, so much, but I hope you won't be disappointed in me, though I ain't anything special, I'm sorry about that, all I got to give you is my love but I got that in spades, an' I wonder what you will be, but I have to tell you something, this is so important baby, you can be anything you want, anything, *you can be better than me, cleverer, luckier, stronger, you have so much potential, maybe I can't give you much, not the fancy stuff you'd deserve, not the stuff that you'd get if my love was money, but I swear I won't let anyone hurt you, never,* never, *and I love you so much*

   – and it didn't understand them but maybe remember because they were good sounds, made it sleep happy protected, the two of them one beat of the blood, always was always will be always.

Acknowledgements

This is my tenth book. That's some kind of achievement unlocked, right? I did it through the help and support of friends, family (actually, humans shouldn't separate those two so much: one is the other and the other is one), my readers, my champions. Thanks to my beta readers Helen, Alyson, Angela; my editor Julie Cohen and proofreader Helen Pryke; my story advisors, particularly Diane Anderson and Yoginee Gokool. Also thanks to Sophie Houlden, game designer and creator of FileKiller (the real software I reference, not the story!)

Thanks to everyone who tells someone else about my books, or writes a short review describing what they enjoyed. To those who buy or gift my books. To those who do good in the world. To those who give me hope.

Thanks to you. I'm sure you know where you fit in the list above.

About The Author

Karl Drinkwater is originally from Manchester but lived in Wales for twenty years, and now calls Scotland his home. He's a full-time author, and was a professional librarian for over twenty-five years. He has degrees in English, Classics, and Information Science.

He writes in multiple genres: his aim is always just to tell a good story. Among his books you'll find elements of literary and contemporary fiction, gritty urban, horror, suspense, paranormal, thriller, sci-fi, romance, social commentary, and more. The end result is interesting and authentic characters, clever and compelling plots, and believable worlds.

When he isn't writing he loves exercise, guitars, computer and board games, the natural environment, animals, social justice, cake, and zombies. Not necessarily in that order.

If you enjoyed this work then please rate it or leave a review on the seller's website or www.goodreads.com. Thank you.

Find Karl Online

Follow Karl using the options below to be informed whenever he publishes a new book.

Website: karldrinkwater.uk
Newsletter: bit.ly/newsletterkd
Facebook: @karlzdrinkwater
Twitter: @karldrinkwater
Instagram: @authorkdrinkwater

Other Titles

LOST SOLACE

Lost Solace

Chasing Solace

LOST TALES OF SOLACE

Helene

Grubane

STANDALONE SUSPENSE

Turner

They Move Below

Harvest Festival

MANCHESTER SUMMER

Cold Fusion 2000

2000 Tunes

CONTEMPORARY SHORT STORIES

It Will Be Quick

COLLECTED EDITIONS

Karl Drinkwater's Horror Collection

Author's Notes

Fire In The Hole

This was difficult to write. By the end I was emotionally wrecked. I felt it again during the rewrite. That's the great thing about being a writer or a reader: you live within someone else for a short while. And I think this is the best thing I've written so far.

The idea for the kidnap came while I was in a shop, in a similar circumstance to the story. I combined that experience with tales my sister had told me about Welsh bothy raves, and some articles I'd read about modern cars which autolock in similar circumstances to my story. I didn't plan much beyond that – I just wanted to improvise and see where it would take me, exactly as the protagonist did.

This was written during the 2016 NaNoWriMo – National Novel Writing Month, which takes place every November. It's set in Aberystwyth, where I lived at the time. All the shops and directions were real.

Recalling The Boy

Written in December 2006, when my nephew was ten. Maybe that day I felt like I'd been too harsh on him: I had always tried to instil a "work before pleasure" habit, where we'd spend half an hour studying something he was having trouble with at school, before we were allowed to play computer games together, or watch a film, or go for a cycle ride.

I didn't think anyone would like this story but my beta readers all voted for me to include it, so here it is.

SenSor OS

I have an intense dislike of EULAs (End-User License Agreements), these things people are forced to agree to and be bound by even though they haven't been read or agreed to. I once did an experiment and copied and pasted into a document a selection of the EULAs that were mashed into my face over a five-month period in 2010. It certainly wasn't every relevant agreement/T&C/licence, and nor was it from some specialist sphere like work. This was just from being a normal person using my PC and installing a few games and bits of software and using some online services. The agreements over that period amounted to 331,993 words, or 1,385 A5 pages of dense single-spaced legalese. No one can realistically be agreeing to all that; if I'd included licences I had to deal with from my work in libraries it would probably have tripled that figure or more.

So we are bound by things we never see, forced to receive updates we may not want, and prevented from doing things that might be benign. That was my mindset when I wrote this in NaNoWriMo 2016, further fuelled by Microsoft failing to activate my reinstallation of Windows. The original title was less subtle: *censrOS*.

I also want to mention an interesting language issue. I love languages. I used to translate Ancient Greek every day, and when I moved to Wales I learnt to speak the lovely Welsh language to a basic conversational level. Since this story is told from the perspective of a Scot, I adopted a light form of Scots language for the protagonist. Scots language (which isn't the same as Scottish Gaelic) is recognised as an indigenous language of Scotland. It has its own vocabulary and rules.

In the 18th century some people tried to Anglicise the language. One of their attempts at this was to add apostrophes wherever letters would exist in English – even though they'd never existed there in Scots. In English the present participle usually ends with "ing", but in Scots it ends with "in", so these people added apostrophes to the end of Scottish words in the mistaken belief that they were English words missing a "g".

This is an example of what is known as the "apologetic apostrophe", and was seen by many as implying Scots was not a separate language, but just a subsidiary form of English. Needless to say, that assumption was offensive to many people in Scotland. The movement to Anglicise Scots language faded away, and apologetic apostrophes are now considered unacceptable. That's why there are no apostrophes in this story at the end of words like glowerin, fuckin etc.

The 6.30 Hole

I wrote this some time between 1999 and 2003, aiming at writing that is almost as sparse and bare as the relationship. It was published as the opening piece in a one-off Aberystwyth anthology called Shoot The Messenger, October 2005. The editor loved it but wanted me to delete some of the ending. That has been restored in a shortened form for this edition.

The story was an idea that came to me as I sat at a table eating a meal with someone, looking out on the street below, as we did every day. And, as writers do, I asked myself: what if ...? I suspect many couples experience a 6.30 hole in their relationship, and if they are lucky they survive it.

Below The Surface

At college I did an extended essay on "island fiction" (mainly Robinson Crusoe, Lord of the Flies, and The Tempest). Since then I'd always wanted to write a shipwreck story. Although this was written in NaNoWriMo 2016, the seeds had been planted years before. I just hadn't got round to tending them. It began as a 220-word outline under four headings: one hour after being washed ashore; one day; one week; one month. I liked the tightness of that structure but it didn't leave much room for character development.

The original island was more of a normal desert island, rather than the flooded rocky outcrop it became as my instinct for horror slipped in. I also considered other story arcs, such as the woman pining for a husband, and her fellow survivor being pleased because he got to hoard supplies, but after her death he realised that being alone was worse; or a predatory man withholding supplies in order to manipulate the woman (edging into thriller territory). But I much prefer the positive message of what I ended up with.

Oh, and Winston finds it hard to believe there would be rafts of plastic out at sea, but he was wrong. There are whole islands of the stuff, polluting the marine environment and poisoning or tangling wildlife.

It Will Be Quick

Written in May 2009. Yes, I sat on these stories for a long time.

Many women I know were kind and brave enough to share their experiences of childbirth. The story came out of that. Some of it was from my mother's recounting of my own birth.

Hell's Bean Curd

Obviously not one of my hard-hitting tales, but sometimes you need a change of mood and gear as a breather. Written in NaNoWriMo 2016, based on an idea I'd had some years earlier and saved as "first aid heart attack.rtf".

In tofu's defence: I love it, and haven't choked yet.

Sweet Nothing

I can't remember when I wrote this, but I sometimes read it out during writing courses I attended as my performance piece (it was an ideal length for that). It won the Writers' Village International Short Fiction Award Summer 2014, a cash sum of £50.

Growing up in the North, I was familiar with the phrase "sweet FA" or "sweet fuck all", meaning "nothing":

"How much did he give you?"

"Sweet FA."

"What a stingy bastard."

The sweet part of the story's title is clear, the other part perhaps relates to the absence of compassion and care.

How I Wonder What You Are

I wrote the story in NaNoWriMo 2016 but the idea came to me many years earlier while cycling in the Highlands with my girlfriend. She went ahead and I temporarily lost sight of her. A white van passed and I suddenly had the idea for this story, fully formed (apart from the ending, which I only had vague ideas for).

The original notes gave it the working name of Highland Horror, but when I started writing it I became aware of rhythm, and the way that nursery rhymes like Twinkle Twinkle Little Star can take on an ominous and repetitive quality (something I exploited in two of the stories from my They Move Below collection). Twinkle Twinkle Little Star led to a better title, by far.

FileKiller

This is a real game. I read about it in an article in 2011, and was scared when I felt an insidious temptation to install it as a challenge. I also wondered what kind of person this FileKiller-type software would appeal to.

The answer came while on a Writing Women's Popular Fiction course at Ty Newydd in 2015, led by authors Julie Cohen and Rowan Coleman. In one of Rowan's sessions we were asked to think of a character and answer some questions from their perspective. This was what I wrote, and it led to the FileKiller protagonist.

- What is your favourite occupation? Winning.
- What is your most treasured possession? Nothing. Everything is a means to an end.
- What or who is the greatest love of your life? Every man is a disappointment.
- What is your favourite journey? Running to work. Favourite, but hates it too. She has to.
- What is your most marked characteristic? Past is irrelevant. The challenge is now.
- What is it that you most dislike? Aimless life or losing. Memories.
- What is your greatest fear? Remembering.
- What is your greatest regret? Having a past.

Cry, Wolf

In February 2012 I attended a Writing In Genre class, and we were given an exercise to take a fairy tale and write it from the perspective of a lesser character. I didn't exactly follow that brief, but was inspired by The Boy Who Cried Wolf.

The first draft was rough, but I read it out at the end of the class, and I did it with conviction. Performance of a piece can sometimes change its reception. One of the other writers in the group blogged about the experience that night, saying:

> *Karl's story was an assault on the psyche of everyone in the room. It was vile, repugnant, out of control, despicable – and deliberately so. At the end of the story, the response was not an intellectual one of "I like what you did with X, but not so keen on Y," rather it was a coming to terms with the emotions we were each feeling, and why we were so appalled, and what it meant for the person in the story. It was an important lesson.*

The Potential

I wrote the first draft of this in 1997 or 1998, whilst working for Manchester Metropolitan University. It was one of those brain splurges that I had to get down on paper, but I didn't think I'd ever do anything with it, and it would get filed or deleted along with many other failed experiments.

Then in 2015 or 2016 I had another look at my sheets of paper, typed it up, and gave it a more fable-like presentation.

Again, I didn't think much of it, so was surprised when my beta readers told me they loved it and I should include it in the collection. So there you go. What do I know, anyway?

Miasma

For many years I studied classics, particularly ancient Greek culture and language. Miasma was blood pollution, bad from bad, whether intention existed or not. It was a dangerous force, continually reworked by the tragedians, and tied to the nightmarish Erinyes; the rituals surrounding animal sacrifice showed the Greek uneasiness at any blood-spilling. Blood pollution worked in cycles. Once the bad things happened they kept happening in the same way – perverted killing, sacrificing and eating. Similar attitudes existed in other cultures, where lowest caste people did jobs that were seen as "ritually impure", anything involving death and blood e.g. execution, undertakers, leatherworkers, butchers. Our society takes a similar approach, trying to hide the guts and any suffering from consumers, so producers can imply it just magically appears on supermarket shelves, with anything unpalatable about the process hidden.

And so I wrote this story, circular like a saw, where everything is connected, and what we do and suffering we cause might impact on the human psyche.

Miasma was published in Secondary Character And Other Stories by Opening Chapter (editor: Barrie Llewelyn; story rights remained with the authors) in August 6, 2015. I attended the book launch and read Miasma to the audience. As expected from a piece like this, I was met with stunned faces at the end. One of the editors of the collection spoke to me afterwards, and said that he'd initially been against my inclusion in the collection, because he wasn't sure what to make of it: but after seeing me read it out so that he could feel the visceral anger pumping in the story, it won him over, and he was glad it was included. He was able to reevaluate what he'd read.

14

A story about a fourteen-year-old boy, set in two thousand and fourteen, just begged to be the fourteenth story of this collection. There's another connection to the number fourteen if you do a sum during the story.

The setting is somewhere near Leek, north-east of Stoke in the Potteries region where I once lived. Place names in the story are a mix of words from real ones around there.

The news reports are all true, and were covered in 2014: English princes shooting wildlife whilst saying wildlife needed protecting, and UK Ministers spending millions to exterminate ducks at the request of Royally sponsored "wildlife protection" organisations. You couldn't make this hypocrisy up. I assume they've now killed all the Ruddy Ducks. It was the perfect backdrop for a story about immigration and attitudes to difference.

Lastly: yes, this is the second story in the collection that ends with someone approaching a door (the other was Sweet Nothing). Doors are the connecting point between inner lives and external lives. Turning points. So they are appropriate for a final link where someone makes a decision or connection that defines them, and gives them identity (which is why it's the first time we hear the Sweet Nothing boy's name).

Balance

This story, written in February 2010, is about a few different things. Some of my readers said they were confused at the end, having thought this was a story set in the past, but then realising it is actually a tale from the future. I refused to make the setting clearer at the start, though, because that's one of the effects I intended. Many people see their historical ancestors as primitive, but history also teaches us that some lessons aren't learnt, and mistakes get repeated, and winning a battle for equality doesn't mean you are safe forever and can rest easy. Justice requires constant effort. Much of my fiction has an undercurrent of cycles repeating if we are not careful, and that can just as easily be a cycle of injustice and cruelty.

Bloodline

An epilogue that eventually evolved out of some of the story titles from this collection, mixed with a soundscape experiment I wrote during a Paula Meehan workshop in August 2005. That experiment was rewritten for this collection during NaNoWriMo 2016. I thought it was important, after seeing so many examples of good and bad humanity, to at least end on a potentially positive message. When the shouting and the rattle of broken dishes comes to a halt, and all we have is silence, we still have choice in what our utterances are.

Lightning Source UK Ltd.
Milton Keynes UK
UKHW011007301020
372510UK00002B/74